YOLONDA'S
Genius

YOLONDA'S
Genius

CAROL FENNER

Aladdin Paperbacks

First Aladdin Paperbacks edition, January 1997
Copyright © 1995 by Carol Fenner

Aladdin Paperbacks
An imprint of Simon & Schuster
Children's Publishing Division
1230 Avenue of the Americas
New York, NY 10020

Also available in a Margaret K. McElderry Books edition.
Designed by Nancy Williams
The text of this book was set in 12-point Baskerville.
Printed and bound in the United States of America

The Library of Congress has cataloged the hardcover edition as follows:

Fenner, Carol
Yolonda's genius / Carol Fenner. — 1st ed.
p.   cm.
Summary: After moving from Chicago to Grand River, Michigan, fifth grader Yolonda, big and strong for her age, determines to prove that her younger brother is not a slow learner but a true musical genius.
[1. Moving, Household—Fiction.   2. Brothers and sisters—Fiction.   3. Genius—Fiction.   4. Musicians—Fiction.   5. Afro-Americans—Fiction.]   I. Title.
PZ7.F342Yo   1995   [Fic]—dc20   94-46962   CIP   AC

This novel is a work of fiction. Names, characters, places, and incidents are either of the author's imagination or are used fictitiously.

ISBN 0-689-82172-7

For Jay

Acknowledgments

I wish to thank the following for valued input that helped me fashion *Yolonda's Genius*:

my husband, Jay Williams, whose appreciation for music deepened my own, who introduced me to the excitement of Chicago's music festivals, whose observations strengthened some critical scenes

my goddaughter, Jessica Rowe, for the Mozart "horrible trills"

my friend Peggy Davis, for her resource clues and neck massages

my great-niece, Becca King, whose comments after reading a marked-up manuscript prompted me to retain deleted sections

my niece Claudia Alexander, who clambered through an early version and gave me new insights

my mother, Esther Gerstenfeld; sister, Faith King; brother, Andrew Fenner; niece Maria King McBreen; for listening, in fits and starts, from the beginning

the city of Chicago for hosting, with gusto, two gigantic and marvelous music festivals annually, blues in June and jazz in September

my friends Carol Shoesmith, speech pathologist and pre-primary-impaired-education specialist, and Kathy Woodrow, a Chapter I director, for their enthusiasm and their interest in Andrew

the six writers in my intrepid writers' group—Bonnie Alkema, Ardyce Czuchna-Curl, Betty Horvath, Ellen Howard, Terri Martin, and Wendy Risk—who lived through Yolonda's and Andrew's trials and celebrations, page by page, and gave me encouragement and advice

my editor, Margaret K. McElderry, whose rare intelligence

and zeal cradled the early manuscript, whose insightful questions and suggestions made revisiting my work a fruitful challenge, whose knowledge of the world into which this book must enter helped smooth its passage

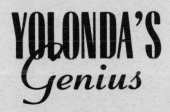

YOLONDA'S Genius

CHAPTER ONE

It was hard to say which terrible thing made their mother decide to finally leave Chicago, where Yolonda and her little brother, Andrew, had lived all their lives. It could have been the fact that both terrible things happened within fourteen hours of each other. The second one wasn't so terrible, really, Yolonda had concluded. Nobody had died, and Andrew was no junkie. It was just maybe the last straw.

The first and really terrible thing was the shooting at school. Willie Meredith was dead and Tyrone had done it. And Yolonda should never have told

Momma. It made Momma think her children were in some new kind of danger. But Yolonda hadn't been able to stop her mouth. Telling her momma had helped settle some of the images—Willie toppling to the floor, Tyrone walking stiffly away between two police officers, her fifth-grade teacher with his bloody arm.

"It looked just like a toy gun, Momma," Yolonda had said. *Why didn't I keep my big mouth shut? Why didn't I wrestle the gun away from Tyrone? I'm bigger.* She'd always wanted to give Tyrone a hug, smile into the warm gleam of his eyes. But she'd stood there thinking it was all some stupid boy joke.

Yolonda's mother was quiet that evening, after Yolonda told her of the shooting at school. She kept going to the window to look down into the street. Yolonda checked the view several times to see what was so interesting and finally decided that her mother was staring through the snow to some other planet. The street below looked beautiful through the snowflakes; the streetlight shone softly on shapes made thick and gentle. But her mother wasn't admiring the transformation.

A little pulse of worry tickled inside Yolonda's big body, but it wasn't until the second terrible thing happened the very next morning that their mother seemed to reach an absolute final decision about leaving Chicago.

*   *   *

"What's that, Andrew?" their mother asked at breakfast. She wore her deep headache frown. Outside it was still snowing, and the street sounds were muffled; the clank of the garbage truck was softened; even a close-by siren sounded thick.

Andrew carefully untangled the tiny packet from the other stuff, dusty stuff he'd had in his pocket forever—since the last blue-jeans wash anyway. Yolonda saw three pennies, a half stick of gum, his harmonica, a folded handkerchief—gray at the creases—a paper clip, and a red shoelace. All of this had been keeping company with some dust balls and the white, wrinkled little packet.

Yolonda grabbed her breath, held it. The packet sure looked like the cocaine some kids bought outside the playground from older kids who acted as mules for small-time pushers. The pushers, it was rumored, answered to Cool Breeze, a big-time drug prince from Jamaica. *Cool Breeze—don't let him look at you long or he can witch you—send his Hundred Gang after you—stick pins in a doll for you to go blind or sicken and die.* Everyone was afraid of Cool Breeze.

Andrew pushed the packet toward his mother. "For your headache," he said. "Boy at school said it makes you feel better."

"What is it?" Their momma picked up the packet with her long, pretty fingers. The headache frown deepened.

"I dunno," said Andrew. "A big boy gave it to me.

3

He said it would make me feel good. But I already felt okay. Maybe it could fix your headache."

Yolonda stifled a groan. She didn't believe all that stuff about Cool Breeze's evil eye, but a part of her wondered if he'd bother to use it on a six-year-old.

"My Lord!" said their mother, staring at the packet. "How long have you had this?"

Andrew examined the stuff from his pocket, thinking. "Longer than the gum," he said.

Their mother took a deep breath and let it out slowly. "Do you know what this is? What I think it is?"

Yolonda could see all the warnings—from their momma, from Aunt Tiny, from TV, from Yolonda herself—suddenly crystalize in Andrew's mind. His eyes, usually a soft toffee color, darkened in his angel face. Probably his teacher at school had done her share of warning, too—even in first grade. *Say no. Don't take candy from a stranger. This is your brain on drugs.*

She saw him shiver. The big boy who'd given him the tiny packet had probably not been so big— fourth, fifth grade—and probably no stranger.

"Is it that bad stuff? Is it that drug stuff?" asked Andrew.

"Oh, Lord," said Andrew's momma. She went to the window. She stared down into the street, hold-

4

ing the tiny packet like something might jump out of it. "Oh, Lord." Shaking her head. Staring at her planet.

Andrew and Yolonda watched from the breakfast table. They waited, each in their own way, for their momma to utter her usual moan: "We've got to get out of this town." But this time, she didn't say a word. She just stared down through the snow at that planet of hers.

Yolonda's pulse of worry returned, rose, and beat against her temples.

She knew that night, when her mother got out her handsome leather briefcase and started going over her résumé, that she was going to find another job—away from Chicago.

Her mother's idea of a great place to live included fresh air, peace and quiet, and trees. She was always talking about growing flowers and owning a barbecue grill that they wouldn't have to chain to the house. Yolonda fretted. Her mother's tastes were definitely limited.

"I don't ever want to move to a place where they can't do double Dutch," she said to the back of her mother's head.

Her momma didn't even turn around. "Better to be a big fish in a little pond," she said, "than a little fish in the ocean."

"I'm already a big fish in these waters," said

Yolonda. Yolonda was big—huge. Tall and heavy and strong. Double Dutch wasn't one of her powers, nor was making friends, but she often stood around watching, hoping the jumpers would need a rope turner. "I'm already a big fish," she repeated.

Her momma laughed. "You got that right, baby," she said.

Yolonda sighed. She wondered unhappily how much time she had to cram in the precious morsels of Chicago living. She suddenly loved her street, her school, the kids who were not her friends. She loved the great public library and the Art Institute of Chicago. How long, she wondered, before her mother found a law firm in another place that needed a paralegal?

What is mom's job? Where is the evidence?

CHAPTER TWO

This is a new place, a strange place, Yolonda thought, and a part of her knew she was dreaming. There was something missing from this place in her dream. It was quiet all around and there was a fresh smell like parks in summer—Grant Park near the fountain when a breeze swept in cool off Lake Michigan. But this quiet didn't belong to Grant Park or any truly familiar place, and Yolonda felt a sadness seeping into her dreaming and realized she was waking up. And realized where she was.

She kept her eyes closed and willed herself back

in Chicago, willed the lively noise from morning streets outside her Chicago window—garbage trucks clanking and the shouts of the workers, the rush and buzz of automobiles, the indistinct thumpings of the family in the next apartment. But the quiet of her dream stayed with her. It was so still that she could hear the birds outside.

The sadness stayed with her, too. So she lay there and waited for it to settle or go away. And while she waited, eyes closed, plump hands curved gently near her cheek, two comforting sounds filled the light spaces in the air. One was her ample stomach growling for breakfast. The other was the sweet sound of her little brother, Andrew, playing on his wooden pipe. He was piping his special waking-up music, a song he'd invented all by himself.

Yolonda's sadness began to ease away. She opened her eyes. It used to be her habit to sleep until she heard Andrew's music. The bright, clear notes had always been her alarm clock back home in Chicago. But ever since they'd moved away, months and months ago, it was her sadness that woke her first—that and the quiet.

Get up, get dressed, sang the sweet roll and pitch of Andrew's pipe. Yolonda sat up. Sunlight was spilling through the trees outside, making moving patterns on the floor of a room she didn't have to share. That was another thing. The morning light didn't stay in the squared-off patterns she'd taken for granted back home in Chicago. It moved all around, and the shadow shapes were soft and blurred, not clear and sharp.

Her mother said they'd all get used to Grand River, Michigan. But the new school still seemed unreal. It wasn't just the newer-looking fifth-grade textbooks—or the work. Some was easier, some tougher; some was just as boring. It would take longer than a few months for Yolonda, accustomed to scenting trouble, to relax. There was no trouble in the air in Grand River—at least no trouble that threatened her life or her lunch money. There was no trouble. There was no nuthin'.

Yolonda threw back the covers to air the bed while she dressed. Then she made it up carefully. Her momma said she made a mean bed.

She could hear her mother outside in the backyard, watering her new plantings. She was growing flowers in their wide, green, clean backyard. They had shade trees and a picnic table and a brand-new unchained barbecue grill. If Andrew left his bike outside, it was still there in the morning. You never needed to be on your toes in this town. Boring.

Before going downstairs to breakfast, Yolonda sneaked into her mother's room. It was a big bedroom with pretty new curtains and a picture view of the quiet street and the trees with their flutter of new spring leaves. Her mother had her own bathroom with peach-colored tiles and little round lights around the wide mirror. Back in Chicago their apartment had cost more and had only had one bathroom.

"My money goes a lot further here in Grand River," Yolonda's momma said now every time she paid the rent. "That's another plus for this town."

Yolonda's eight-dollar allowance went further in Grand River, too. She had tried to work a cost-of-living increase out of her momma during the confusion of moving four months ago, but her momma had just raised her eyebrows and then laughed. "Trying to take advantage of your poor, broke momma? You are one smart girl, Yolonda. But your momma's still smarter. You should be getting a *decrease* for this town." Yolonda had quickly dropped the subject.

On the peach-colored bathroom counter were her momma's creams and powders, her perfumed soaps and colognes. Yolonda carefully opened a blue jar of moisturizer and dabbed some on her face, then smoothed it in.

She'd started primping back in Chicago when she'd begun to fall in love with Tyrone and dream about the bright glint of his eyes. Once he'd commented, "You sure smell good, Londa," and she had savored his voice, that moment, the high shine of his eyes for weeks.

Now she reached for her mother's Giorgio. The perfume cost a hundred seventy dollars an ounce, so her mother only bought the cologne. Yolonda dabbed some on her handkerchief to rub on her throat later. She stuffed the handkerchief into her backpack. Her mother would freak out if she smelled it on her. The cologne itself cost forty bucks. *Poor broke Momma—yeah.*

Even though the Tyrone she'd been so crazy about was gone from her life, the habit of attracting him remained. Besides, in this nerdy hick school, she was establishing her image of worldly superiority. Giorgio helped.

As she descended the stairs, the rich smell of bacon filled her nostrils. Good, thought Yolonda. She loved bacon—and the thick smell would cancel any traces of Giorgio.

Andrew was already at the kitchen table, sitting with his back to the sun, which, softened by breezy curtains, spilled into the room. He looked like a thin little angel to Yolonda. He was listening intently to something. Their mother, an apron over her business suit, was turning the sizzling bacon. And there were pancakes browning on the griddle.

Andrew picked up his ever-present harmonica and played a strange buzzing, cracking sound, his cheeks puffing out like plums.

"What's that?" asked Yolonda as she shoved herself into a chair.

"The bacon," said Andrew, a little indignant that she hadn't recognized the sound of bacon on his harmonica.

"Oh, yeah. Yeah. I see," said Yolonda. Now that he'd named it, the sound *did* have the sizzle of bacon. Like some paintings didn't make sense until you read the title.

"Now I'm trying to hear the pancakes," said Andrew.

"You can stop playing, Andrew," said their mother, placing plates before each of them. "You can start eating."

No one had to tell Yolonda to start. The rich scent of almond flavoring rose with the heat from pancakes browned in beautiful patterns. She already knew she wanted seconds before she even started on firsts.

"No seconds, Yolonda," said her mother, reading her mind. "And see that Andrew eats his. I'm already late."

As her mother hurried out the door to her car, she hollered back. "Make sure he eats, Yolonda. Don't you eat his breakfast for him."

"All right!" Yolonda yelled back in her meanest voice. Her mother was in too big a hurry to challenge her rudeness now. Yolonda decided not to tell her that she was still wearing her apron. Anyway, Andrew wouldn't eat all his pancakes, and Yolonda wasn't about to let them go to waste.

They waited for the school bus at their corner. Each morning Yolonda steeled herself for the ride. She hadn't yet figured out how to handle these whispering girls or the sniggering boys with their stage-whisper slurs about her big body. The taunts came from black kids as well as white kids.

Back in Chicago, most of the kids in her school, in her neighborhood, were black. Everyone had learned not to name-call or bait her. Even older boys steered clear. But that was in the freedom of the street, where Yolonda could unleash her sharp tongue and use her powerful arms, her great size, to scare off any abuse.

Here you had to be careful. The bus driver could turn you in for fighting. The atmosphere, with more white kids than black, was tame and murky. Yolonda studied it carefully.

So far, she had kept to herself. She read on the bus, ignoring "Hey, whale, you'll break the seat," hurled like a blade from behind. She made her silence a brick wall and kept on reading. She reviewed last night's homework or buried herself in a novel, but a part of her mind noted who the offender was. You wait, said that part of her mind to comfort her. You wait.

This morning she realized with dismay that, in her guilty rush to finish the rest of Andrew's pancakes, she had left *Island of the Blue Dolphins* on a chair.

Well, she could look over her homework. She always did her homework. Being a good student was easier in Grand River than in Chicago. You didn't have to camouflage being school-smart here. In Chicago it was uncool to get good grades—not a black thing. *Who you think you are?*

When the bus came, she had her homework out of her backpack. The seats up front were occupied, and she didn't want to push down the narrow aisle past everyone to the seats in the back. The maniacs sat in the back. She decided to stand. This bus driver was easygoing; he might not make her sit if she was quiet.

There was a small space on one seat near the window, and she said gruffly to Andrew, "Sit." Clutching his harmonica, her brother eased over a third grader and sat.

Yolonda stood holding on to the edge of a seat in the second row. She held her homework toward the light, the better to read her pretty, slanted handwriting. She dotted her *i*'s with tiny circles and ended every sentence in a curled sweep.

"Sit down, whale. You're breakin' the floor," a voice hissed at her from somewhere midbus. Gasps, giggles, and guffaws erupted around her. Yolonda straightened her back, keeping her eyes on her homework. Her mind searched the boys' voices she knew. White boy, definitely. Was it dumb George? Was it Danny with his daddy longlegs and pimpled cheeks? Gerard, smart and sly in his too-white shirt?

"Hey, whale!"

Whales surfaced in Yolonda's mind. *Their big gray heads were slapped by little waves, their small eyes peering.*

Yolonda turned her face toward the voice. Danny-longlegs still had his hand cupped around his mouth, his legs splayed out in the aisle.

Slowly Yolonda edged her way back to his seat. He sat slumped, with a smirk on his face, long legs hogging the narrow space.

"What do you know about whales, blisterface?" asked Yolonda softly. She looked down at him. "You don't know diddly, do you?"

Danny shifted uneasily in his seat, but slid an angry glance up at her.

The whales peered from their little eyes. Then they spouted up beautiful gushes of water like the fountain in Grant Park.

Yolonda looked into Danny's reddening face. "Whales are the most remarkable mammals in the ocean—all five oceans."

Danny's lip curled, but before he could make any reply, Yolonda carefully lifted her solid right foot and brought it squarely and gently down over Danny-longlegs's huge running shoe. She watched his face pale under the frozen smirk as she slowly settled her weight onto his foot.

"Whales sing to one another through hundreds of miles of water. They have a high keening sound and a low dirgelike sound."

"Get off my effin' foot, you cow," muttered Danny through his teeth. There was a giggle from behind them.

"Right," said Yolonda, her voice gooey with mock praise, "the female whale is called a cow. Didn't know a farmer boy like you was so well informed." And Yolonda leaned her weight deeper into his foot.

He grimaced in pain and shot a glance at the bus driver.

"The music whales make is found to be beautiful, and people make recordings of it. It is found to be powerful, and musicians create background music for it."

His face went blank and she knew she was mesmerizing him. She knew he didn't want to sound stupid in front of his friends and the girls in back. She knew a struggle against her foot would look uncool.

She increased the pressure on his toes by twisting away from him and pretending to review her homework again.

"Get off my effin' foot!" His anger had a begging sound, and Yolonda was gratified by loud giggling and snorts of laughter from the back of the bus.

"Keep it down to a dull roar, kids," the bus driver called good-naturedly without taking his eyes off the road.

The whales sank, lifting their tails high above the water like a signal. Deep in the ocean, their voices sent out a high swelling cry, sharing their message of victory for a hundred miles.

Although she was prepared to confront Danny-longlegs when the bus reached the school, he brushed past her in a hurry, heading for his room.

Yolonda watched Andrew trudge off to his first-grade class, slipping his harmonica into his back pocket. Andrew didn't do well in school like Yolonda. He couldn't even read one word yet and had to attend a special reading class for slow learners. He didn't make friends easily, but he didn't make enemies either.

"Oh, that was really cool." The voice at her

elbow was manlike, gruff. When she turned, Yolonda was surprised to find herself looking down into a small, pale girl's face.

"Hi. I'm Shirley Piper," said the man voice. All of this Shirley person was small except for her voice and her large, pale blue eyes whirling behind the thickest glasses Yolonda had ever seen—whirling, yes, and twitching behind the thick lenses.

"You were really something," said the Shirley person. "What else do you do?" Then she laughed, a kind of deep, dry ha-ha-ha-hacking laugh.

"I play the piano," said Yolonda demurely, "mostly classical like Mozart. I get straight A's." She stared at the Shirley person. "I look after my kid brother. I do the laundry for our whole family. I can make cake from scratch."

Then Yolonda decided to lie. "I do double Dutch." She watched Shirley's face for traces of disbelief. None. "I can do 'Teddy Bear.' And 'Pepper'—with the right rope turners, of course."

Shirley Piper's eyes whirled admiringly. "That bit about the whales. I loved the narrative you gave Danny about the whales. Did you memorize it or are you a genius?"

"No," said Yolonda. She was surprised at the word *narrative*. "I didn't really memorize that. I just *knew* it." She could barely remember what she'd said to Danny-longlegs—just the image in her head of majestic whales. She checked Shirley out again. "What do *you* do?" she asked.

"Oh, I don't have all your talents," said Shirley in her gruff voice. "I read a lot, but I barely find enough time to study. My A's aren't straight. More like crooked A's. They sort of hump over the B's and a C or two." She ha-ha'd again. "I can't even turn the ropes for double Dutch."

"Don't feel bad," said Yolonda, suddenly generous. "Turning the ropes correctly is an art—it's really hard."

The bell rang and they both turned hurriedly toward the school.

"You have to have good rhythm and your partner has to be in sync with you. You know, really good vibes," hollered Yolonda after Shirley's scurrying figure. Without looking around, the Shirley person flapped her hand in a wave.

Well, I've impressed one person in this burg at least, thought Yolonda, even if she has a man voice and whirlygig eyes. Even if she is whiter than white.

She only felt slightly guilty about her lie. She was sure that she could do "Teddy Bear" here among these countrified kids. It looked a lot slower and easier. They didn't know diddly about double Dutch in this burg, even though they worked at it. She'd seen black girls here teaching white girls "the ropes." She wasn't sure black people and white people could get it together right. And no one here did it like they did back on the streets of Chicago. No one could fly in and out of the whirr-slap of ropes like the Chicago girls, who had never been her friends, who hardly ever let her turn the ropes. No one here had such quick, light feet and legs like hot motor pistons. Yolonda had to admit to herself that "Pepper" was too wildly fast anywhere for someone her size to master. That was a bigger lie.

She'd told another sort-of lie to the Shirley person. She'd never had good enough vibes with anyone to turn the ropes in perfect rhythm. She was always criticizing her partner before they even started. "You're too short," or, belligerently, "You never done this before?"

Only once had she seen rope turning done in perfect sync. In Chicago. On the playground at recess. The girls had been close in size and they moved their arms in an easy, relaxed way—turning, turning, their eyes fixed, not on each other, but sort of out of focus, listening—the way Andrew did all the time. When the recess bell had rung, the partners had laughed and slapped gently at each other with pleasure, then wound up the ropes. They had gone back into the school building with their arms slung across each other's shoulders.

For a while, Yolonda liked to remember that. She liked to pretend that those girls had been her friends.

CHAPTER THREE

"Now, Andrew, we can't play with our harmonica when we're reading," said Miss Gilluly. She sat next to him at the little round table. She had a kind voice. "We must put the harmonica and other toys away so we can concentrate on the task at hand."

Andrew looked at the bright page in front of him across which marched a regiment of black marks. He clutched the harmonica and his chin went stubborn. Then he gave up. She might take his harmonica away from him. He'd seen that happen to others before. LaToya French had been made to put her push-wind racing car on the teacher's desk for the whole reading lesson. Stacey Goldstein's drinking-wetting doll had wet 2-percent milk all over her workbook. She couldn't ever bring that doll to school again.

Andrew carefully slid the harmonica into his back pocket, the one farthest from Miss Gilluly. He looked again at the bright page with the black marks. He was supposed to tell this woman what the marks meant. They were some sort of code people used instead of talking. He didn't really care what the message was because above the marks was a picture of some boring-looking kids playing in a sandbox. He knew what they were doing and what they were saying and he knew he wouldn't even want to play with them. They would probably get into an argument over the little red truck in the picture. There were two white kids in the picture and two colored brown. The brown ones didn't look like him or any other blacks kids he knew. They looked like white kids colored brown. He didn't want to play with them at all.

"Can you tell me what the first word says, Andrew?" asked Miss Gilluly.

Andrew hunched down and looked at his hands. His hands already missed the harmonica, and his mouth itched to play a tune. *No, no,* he would play on the harmonica. *This is stupid,* he would play on his harmonica. Then he might imitate Miss

Gilluly's voice—low and kind and floaty. Or he might simply fly away on his harmonica and leave Miss Gilluly with her mouth like an *O*.

Miss Gilluly sighed and took away the book. She slipped _____ of Andrew. The pictur___ ___ s foot on a ball. Andre___ ___ harmonica, but it was in ___ ___ stared at the picture. U___ ___ few of the black code m___ ___

"Car___ ___ e picture?" asked Miss Gilluly. It was so obvious what was in the picture that Andrew thought Miss Gilluly must mean that something he couldn't see was hidden in the lines of the picture—like the puzzles on the comics page of the newspaper that Yolonda liked to do. Find the hidden faces. So Andrew looked real hard for hidden faces in the picture.

"What do you see there, Andrew?" asked Miss Gilluly a little impatiently.

I hate this reading, thought Andrew, and he ached for his harmonica. He couldn't see any hidden faces, so he just put his head down on the picture. I'm the hidden face, he thought, and this made him smile.

"What's so funny?" asked Miss Gilluly, and Andrew could tell that she was upset. "There's nothing funny in that picture!"

Andrew made his mind fly up and away. Bark-bark, he heard in his head. Inside his mind he bounced the ball, and the little puppy jumped in such a funny way that Andrew wanted to laugh, but he didn't want to make Miss Gilluly madder, so he shut his eyes and he listened to the sound a ball makes bouncing, a dog makes jumping. Thump-ump. Bark-bark.

In her classroom, Yolonda took her seat near the front, where she could exert a certain amount of control. She didn't sit in the first seat, which, she'd noticed way back in third grade, the teacher often stared over. She had requested the third seat, third row, claiming she had a peripheral-vision problem and couldn't see the board unless she was square in front of it and not too close. But she really wanted to be in line with Mr. Johnkoski's eyes when he stood facing the class. That way all Yolonda had to do was modestly raise her hand to get called on. And, besides the answer to Mr. Johnkoski's questions, she almost always had an accompanying comment. Yolonda liked Mr. Johnkoski better than any teacher she'd had since first grade.

"Who can name the vertebrates?" asked Mr. Johnkoski as the class settled down. "Yolonda?"

Yolonda worked herself out of her seat and

stood. "Animals with a backbone are called vertebrates. The five main groups of vertebrates are fish, amphibians, reptiles, birds, and mammals."

"That's correct, Yolonda."

"Humans are mammals. It is believed that we humans all developed out of apes. There are some religions that don't accept this as a fact. They don't believe that we all came from the ape family. They say we all came from Adam and Eve, not a hairy ape." There was some snickering. Yolonda turned in the direction of the snickers. "There are some people who resemble apes more than others." She paused, looking about her. "They look like apes and they sound like apes." The snickers exploded all around the room. "That's proof enough for me."

She stopped and glared, folded her hands across her stomach. "Any questions?"

There never were. Just awed silence.

Then someone piped up, "Teacher's pet!" from the back of the room, breaking the spell.

Yolonda sat down.

"Teacher's pet elephant," snorted someone else, which sent off a wave of snickers and giggles. Yolonda turned to study the back of the room with contempt.

Mr. Johnkoski ignored the hilarity. "What distinguishes mammals from the other groups?" he asked. A few hands shot up. Yolonda didn't want to think about vertebrates right now, but she raised her hand anyway. She knew Mr. J wouldn't call on her again until map study.

Stuffed into the third seat, third row, Yolonda slipped out her homework map with the states in different colors. She arranged her books in the order of her lessons, folded her hands, and allowed her mind to dwell on her encounter with the Shirley person.

How come she'd never noticed her before? Her gruff voice alone was enough to make her stand out. Maybe she didn't ordinarily talk much. If she didn't say much, probably no one would notice her small shape or her whirlygig eyes.

"Are you a genius?" she'd asked Yolonda.

After school, Andrew wanted to watch the skaters on Asphalt Hill. Yolonda often left him at the skateboard park when she had errands to run or wanted to stay at school to help a teacher. The Hill, as it was called by the skateboard jocks, was a series of mounds and ramps, curves and slants, and long, smooth stretches where you could gain speed or do platform tricks.

Andrew liked the grinding, swift sounds the boards made, mixed with the shouts and grunts and cheers of the skaters—the breathing, the yelps at a spill.

It was better to make skateboarding music with his harmonica, but sometimes, when a boy flew through the air on his board and hung there for a long moment, Andrew longed for the sweet, clear note of his little wooden pipe. Sometimes he wished he had two mouths so that he could play both instruments at once.

Some junior-high kids hung out along the edge of the Hill. Yolonda had pointed them out to Andrew with a warning finger. "Pushers, Andrew," she had told him. "Don't take any of those little death packets from them—from anyone."

Andrew thought that, if he had two mouths, he could play the sound of the cocaine packets— maybe low, friendly chords like the smile of the big boy back in Chicago who'd given him the white packet. Play it warm on his harmonica. Then bring out the pipe and blow a high siren screech— choke it and send it off pitch.

He'd seen older students with unfocused eyes who looked as though they were hanging on the edge of something about to tip over. The sound of a skateboard or a cheer didn't seem to reach them.

There used to be a boy from his class who hung out around the junior-high kids on Asphalt Hill. One afternoon, this boy had whined in the boys' bathroom about not being able to go to the toilet because his skin hurt so much. He wailed over and over that he couldn't undo his pants because his skin was killing him. He kept saying over and over, "I can't, Momma. I can't!" He had cried out in such pain that Andrew had run back to his classroom.

"Troy's sick in the bathroom," Andrew had told Mrs. Post. "His skin hurts," he'd added, and Mrs. Post's head had jerked erect. Andrew had watched her hurry out of the room.

Later Andrew had seen Troy being carried down the hall by Mrs. Post and the principal. Troy was jerking and crying, "I can't! Oh, Momma, I can't!"

Troy hadn't been back to school. Mrs. Post had spent the entire afternoon discussing drugs and what had happened to Troy. She had asked the kids if they knew where Troy might have gotten the drugs. Nobody had said anything even though everybody knew about the junior-high kids who hung out around Asphalt Hill.

Andrew couldn't understand why anyone would want to change their eyes so that they couldn't see and, worse yet, change their ears so that they couldn't hear everything. And change their skin so that it hurt.

I can't. I can't! Andrew played on his harmonica as he watched the pushers joking with younger kids by Asphalt Hill. *Oh, Momma. I can't!* Several kids turned around in alarm at the harmonica's cry.

Then Andrew played a sound like his mother calling him, calling him angrily, like the time he'd tried to cross the street by himself.

"Andrew! Get back here this instant!" Her voice had been really more scared than angry, but insistent and powerful.

Andrew! Get back here this instant! played Andrew. He was only mildly surprised when a second-grade boy standing with the group by the junior-high kids lifted his head, startled, shook it, then backed away from the group.

"What's the matter, Karl?" someone asked the boy.

"I thought I heard somebody call me," the boy answered with a bewildered tuck of his head.

CHAPTER FOUR

"Yolonda! Yoh-lon-daah! Big as a Honda!"

The three grinning fifth-grade boys braced themselves, ready to run. Yolonda turned and made her eyes go mean. Then, wordless, she marched toward them. The trio whirled, yelping laughter, and sped across the street, pushing past the crossing guard in her red belt.

Yolonda undid her backpack as she waited to cross. She hoisted it down and began to swing it back and forth.

"Hurry up," she ordered the crossing guard, a

tall, skinny, blond girl. "I can't stand here all day. Get this show on the road."

"*I'm* the crossing guard, not you, Yolonda," squealed the guard. "*I* say when."

"When, then?" growled Yolonda, swinging her backpack like a mace.

"Now," said the girl shrilly. "Now you can cross."

Yolonda's three tormentors had stopped running and were waiting in a doorway. When she was in the middle of the street, they chanted again, "Yolonda! Yoh-lon-daah! Big as a Honda!"

Yolonda marked her enemies well. One was a black kid with ashy skin; one was a hulk and the class dummy; the tallest was pale, pale with a pretty, pimply face.

When she reached the curb, she stopped and forced herself to look thoughtfully into the sky as if she were watching a parachute descend. Keeping her eyes turned upward, she placed her backpack on the ground. Then she stood up and shaded her eyes. She let her mouth drop open.

At the corner of her vision, she could tell that the boys now stood gaping into the sky, too. There wasn't even a cloud.

"Wow!" cried Yolonda, all pretense. Then she whipped around and faced the boys. "What's up there, an invisible flying saucer?" she hollered. When they turned in surprise toward her, she yelled gleefully, "*Gotcha!* Gotcha, dumb nerdwiks."

She bent down, nimbly for someone so round, and picked up her books again. She didn't even turn to look at the three stunned boys. Stately and victorious, she moved back across the street. Now she could get down to business.

She had another reason, besides research or checking out books, to visit the public library this afternoon. It quickened her step.

Usually she had Andrew with her and she would leave him in the children's room, where there was a storytelling hour. Andrew liked to hear stories. Today, however, Andrew wanted to watch the skateboarders and, after Yolonda had again pointed out the junior-high pushers with her usual warnings and made him promise to wait right there for her, she'd headed off alone for the library.

"Londa goin' to the 'brary," Tyrone used to tease a hundred years ago back in Chicago. Her momma had never worried about her daughter taking the city bus downtown. Andrew had a babysitter then, and her mother always said, "No one gonna tackle with Yolonda. Unless they want their heads busted."

The public library in Grand River wasn't far from school. Yolonda could walk. It was a big, old building on a corner, with a modern addition that stretched almost a block. Yolonda had to admit it was really a good library. She haunted it—even on weekends, came to "stuff her head," as her momma called it. She knew the inside well, knew the side door would take her where she wanted to go. But she chose to climb the wide steps instead and go through the high arched doorway. She made her big body go proud and queenly as she walked into the well-lit quiet. She loved the smell of the books, old and new, and the careful silence there.

Once inside, she made a beeline for the reference section, where a huge dictionary lay on a stand. She flipped open the pages to the *G*'s.

Her plump, dimpled finger traced down the left side of the page of *ge* words.

genip, genipap, genit., genital, genitalia . . . She paused to read this one even though it wasn't the word she wanted: "The reproductive organs, especially the external sex organs."

It always slightly surprised Yolonda to find this kind of information in such a respectable book. But, after all, it was an adult dictionary. It had thin, thin paper, not like the school dictionaries. It had a lot more words than the school dictionary—interesting words like *genitalia*.

Yolonda felt in her jacket for her chocolate bar. You weren't supposed to eat anything in the library, but Yolonda always sneaked in a chocolate bar. Eating and reading were great together. With the comfortable warmth of melting chocolate in her mouth and the comfortable feel of a book in her hands, Yolonda was in heaven.

She read a lot standing in the adult stacks. She liked the stark bright words of poets. She pulled out books whose titles intrigued her. She read sexy adult books until her own breathing embarrassed her. Because she was tall for her age, she could pretend, with her face turned inward toward the shelves, that she was an adult.

But today she hadn't put that task on herself. Today it was important to find out what *genius* meant. She wanted a better definition than the one in her school dictionary, which said merely, "genius, n. 1: great natural ability. 2: a very gifted person." What a pale, insipid definition. Who made these stupid dictionaries for kids? Idiots?

The only problem with the adult dictionary was that she usually got sidetracked. But not today. Today she would tackle a nagging question. Was she or was she not a genius?

Genitor. That one was too good to pass up. "1: One who begets or creates. 2: A natural father . . ." Yolonda speculated about her genitor, whom she could only remember sometimes. She'd been five when he'd drowned in a storm while fishing on Lake Michigan.

"I can hardly remember my genitor," she mused aloud, testing the word in her mouth. Her mind drifted.

But not for long. There was *genius*. Two words beyond. She closed her eyes and prayed. Do I want to be? Do I? So what if I'm not. She took another bite of her chocolate bar. She was hoping the word *genius* would mean something about wanting to know, being hungry to know things, wanting to shine brighter than anyone.

"Genius. 1.a. Exceptional or transcendent intellectual and creative power."

Like God, she thought, making the universe. Well, I'm sure enough not God.

She knew she was pretty smart when measured up against most of the yo-yos in her class. She could talk like her teacher and use long words that most teachers didn't even use. She wasn't sure she was *exceptional*—or if she had "transcendent intellectual and creative power." She would have to look up *transcendent*. That would be a good new word to surprise Mr. J with.

Next under *genius* she read, "A natural talent or inclination." Like the school dictionary. Maybe this was where those fools got the definition. However, she considered it. She wasn't sure her abilities were so natural. It seemed to her she worked hard at class work and at figuring out what would earn praise and admiration in school from those who counted. She wasn't sure a genius would go to all that trouble to identify those who counted.

Those who counted were most teachers and the principal. Not the kids lounging against the wall at recess, cupping cigarettes. Not the game jocks shooting baskets, or the lively rope jumpers, or the clusters of whispering ninnies. They don't know diddly nuthin', thought Yolonda.

Then the next statement in the dictionary grabbed her interest. A man called John Hersey had said, "True genius rearranges old material in a way never seen before." The words startled her. Yolonda's mind, caught off guard, began to click and whir.

". . . rearranges old material in a way never seen before." Or, clicked her mind, rearranges old material in a way never *heard* before.

"Andrew!" said Yolonda with a gasp of disappointed wonder. "Andrew is the genius in the family!" Then she shook her head to chase away such an idea. "What am I saying?" she muttered. "He can't even read yet." She grabbed a bite of the chocolate bar. But the knowledge crept across the sweetness melting in her mouth, muting the taste.

She stood there for a long time, her finger on *genius*. She was so accustomed to the things Andrew could do that she never really noticed them. Everyone was always more concerned about what Andrew *couldn't* do—like taking forever to learn to talk. And Yolonda remembered the fuss over why baby Andrew wasn't walking. Other kids his age were toddling bowlegged from chair to chair, and Andrew sat contentedly blowing sounds from his harmonica. It had never mattered to Yolonda that Andrew didn't learn regular things quickly. He was an angel-faced, serious little boy and the only person Yolonda felt great tenderness toward.

Now, suddenly, she thought of the things this angel-faced boy *could* do. If there was music on the TV or the blaster, he could keep it company by beating out a rhythm on anything—his knees, a table, a wall. Or he would play a sweet line of sound on his harmonica just underneath the music, like water under a bridge. He played people's voices—an argument, cries of surprise, hushed conversation. The harmonica lived in his pocket. He fell asleep with it in his hand.

"That's Andrew!" cried Yolonda aloud in the public library when she reread the part about true genius rearranging old material. "A true genius! No wonder no one understands him. They're not smart enough!"

Her mind traveled. Images from long ago slipped slow-motion through her head. *Baby*

Andrew's face is all screwed up with crying. "Poor little tyke," someone says. Her genitor? A crib is in the living room of a place Yolonda remembers only in snatches. "Poor little tyke." Her father's big shape bends over the crib, steam-shovel arms scoop up the baby. "We can't pick him up every time he cries, Deuce." Her mother's voice. There is sunlight coming through windows that seem high up. Yolonda runs. She has new shoes on her four-year-old feet. The shoes click against the floor. She runs and leans against her father's leg, pulling on the trousers, wanting to be picked up, too—shoveled up into those big, sweet arms.

She didn't remember the moment her father had given her baby brother the harmonica. He was still in his crib, though. She remembered his baby mouth sucking on it, eyes scrunched shut. He was teething, her daddy had said. He gave him the harmonica to quiet the crying. Andrew sucked on it and breathed through it, making bubbly notes slide out. Then he listened. Then he did it again.

As she stood at the dictionary, a laugh came clear into Yolonda's mind—her daddy's—and then his whole warm face slipped like a surprise present into her memory. No one ever laughed like her daddy. He had laughed at the notes stopping Andrew's whimper. An old sorrow ached in Yolonda. That's all we got of him, she thought. I got remembering his laugh. Andrew got his harmonica.

It was an old harmonica even back when Andrew was a baby. Daddy called it a mouth harp. It had MARINE BAND embossed into the shiny metal outside and ten square holes in the wood front.

"Youngest harp man in history," Daddy had bragged happily.

That was the beginning of Andrew's music, thought Yolonda, standing with her finger on a page of the dictionary. The rest all just happened so slowly that nobody paid it too much attention. Andrew's harmonica, his pipe, his feet tapping, fingers drumming were all a part of him like his skin.

She closed the dictionary. She would not stay at the library to do her homework or collect any extra relevant facts to fracture her class with. A guilty worry over Andrew had begun to pester her. She hurried from the library and headed back to Asphalt Hill. For some reason her brother seemed more vulnerable now that she'd recognized his gift. She imagined a kidnapping—or a car accident. *She'd told him to stay put*.

But Andrew was there almost where she'd left him, sitting under a tree with a second-grade blond kid named Karl.

"Let's get goin'," she said, her voice gruff with

relief. "We got a long walk home." Then she reached into her pocket, where she had a spare chocolate bar. She broke it in half and gave one piece to Andrew. "Let's get goin'." And she marched off like a troop commander. She looked back briefly when she reached the street. Andrew was dividing his half of the chocolate bar with the kid named Karl.

It would take a good thirty-five minutes to reach their block. Andrew tagged along behind her, every once in a while blowing a sound or two on his harmonica. She waited patiently for him at every corner. When they reached their street, Fremont Street, she paused and said to him, "Did you know? You're a genius."

Andrew looked at her squarely, studied her face for a long moment. Finally he said, "I am not. I'm Andrew." His voice was very sure and he looked only faintly insulted at her name-calling.

CHAPTER FIVE

Yolonda was surprised the next morning when she climbed aboard the bus and found that Shirley Piper of the whirling eyes had saved her a seat. On the aisle and in the first row, the seat had plenty of room for Yolonda.

"I'm one of the first to get on the bus," Shirley informed Yolonda in a gravelly whisper. "I'll save this seat for you tomorrow, too."

"Yeah. Thanks," said Yolonda. But she thought suspiciously, Wonder what she wants.

"I like the window seat up front so I can check out the kids getting on," said the Shirley person.

"You can tell by the way they look what kind of day they're going to have."

The bus lurched forward and a boy who had leaned whispering across the aisle fell out of his seat.

"Like him." Shirley nodded at the embarrassed kid, scrambling to his seat amid hoots and laughter.

"Oh, yeah?" said Yolonda. "What kind of day am I going to have?"

Shirley turned her pale, flickering blue eyes on Yolonda. She studied her awhile, eyes twitching furiously behind the thick lenses. "Lousy," she said. But then she laughed her ha-ha-ha-hacking laugh. "Just kidding. You don't have lousy days."

"You're weird," snorted Yolonda.

"You are, too," said Shirley, "but very interesting—very intelligent."

"Yeah, well, my little brother's a genius," announced Yolonda. Then she bit her tongue. She hadn't even discussed it with her mother yet. Why was she telling this undernourished girl anything?

"The little thin boy with the harmonica? That's your brother? He's so angelic-looking. You don't look anything alike." Shirley giggled, a low throaty sound. "I don't mean that you look like the devil." Then she giggled again. "I don't know what's making me make these jokes."

"What jokes?" commented Yolonda sourly.

Shirley sobered immediately. "Well, if he's a genius, then you do resemble each other," she said. Her man voice took on a very pleasant sound in Yolonda's ears.

"'True genius rearranges old material in a way never seen before,'" quoted Yolonda, turning to look at the Shirley person. The blue eyes were whirling with admiration.

Under the grinding rumble of the bus and the racket of kids around her, Yolonda confided. "Don't tell anyone. No one knows he's a genius except me. But now you know, and I don't know why I told you. Not even my mom knows. And Andrew doesn't understand. He can't read yet and he might get teased. They don't know he's a genius at school. They didn't know in Chicago either." She looked at Shirley, testing her interest. Then she added, "You have to be pretty smart to recognize a true genius."

"You told me because you need someone to tell stuff like that to," said Shirley. "You need to share your innermost thoughts with someone. Everybody does."

"Oh, yeah," snorted Yolonda. "Who do you share yours with?"

Shirley-whirley's face fell. She dropped nervous lids over her flickering eyes and looked at her lap.

Yolonda was surprised to find herself feeling bad.

She softened her voice and said, "I got good ears in case you got something you want to discuss."

"What I thought is . . . ," began the Shirley person hopefully. "What I thought is, you could teach me to turn double Dutch."

Yolonda was stunned. Her lie had come back to attack her.

"Don't have the rope," she stalled.

"I've got the rope," said Shirley, brightening eagerly.

Yolonda's mind churned. "Tell you what," she finally responded. "Let's start with cake. I'll show you how to bake a cake from scratch."

Later, as she walked through the noisy hallway to her locker, she was angry with herself for sharing Andrew's genius with Shirley-whirley. "Why can't I keep my big mouth shut," she muttered under her breath. But on the way to her classroom, Yolonda considered Shirley Piper again. It wouldn't hurt to show her about cake baking. Yolonda's momma didn't usually allow cake in the house—just on special days like birthdays and holidays. "You don't need a lot of cake, Yolonda." But her mother wanted Yolonda to make friends. She was always on Yolonda's case about making friends.

Now Yolonda had the Shirley person for an excuse to bake a cake, and her mouth began to water as she sent cakes through her memory, choosing first a lemon pudding cake with orange cream icing—little flecks of grated orange rind sprinkled about. Then she dreamed a German chocolate cake with all the lovely pecan frosting oozing between the layers. Yeah! But how about a tall, cottony angel food you could pull apart with your hands and dip in melted black-raspberry jam and fresh-whipped cream?

Her Aunt Tiny had taught her to bake. Aunt Tiny was her father's sister. She'd taught Yolonda to read, too, even before she went to school. Aunt Tiny used to live just two blocks over from their street in Chicago. Thinking about cake made Yolonda hungry, but thinking about Aunt Tiny made her lonesome.

"Pleasingly plump," her three-hundred-pound Aunt Tiny called Yolonda. "*I'm* fat," Aunt Tiny would say, rolling her head around proudly on her several chins. "Yolonda—now Yolonda is only pleasingly plump."

Yolonda had loved to visit her aunt. If her momma had to work late, Yolonda would take Andrew and go spend the evening there.

Aunt Tiny had a laugh as rich and flaky as biscuits and gravy. She wore gorgeous clothes—reds so bright and whites so pure and spanking clean. She would fix ribs, baking them slow in the oven, and serve them with red beans and steaming rice. She cooked the beans slow, too, with giant slabs of clove-studded onion.

Tiny's hands were pretty as Momma's, only her nails were very long, squared-off at the tips, and polished a shiny red. She ate with delicate bites, nibbling daintily, mincing her way through rib after rib, wiping her mouth with her napkin, not getting any of the barbecue sauce on her blindingly white slacks. She smelled wonderfully of perfume and food. When she surrounded Yolonda in a big, soft hug, Yolonda could have stayed there forever, inhaling Aunt Tiny's sweetness.

Yolonda was jolted from her reverie by the late bell. As she marched toward her room she considered carrot cake: spices, nuts, and raisins—moist— thick maple icing piled and spread in sugary whirls. She glanced hungrily at her watch. Three and a half hours until lunch. She would survive on a chocolate bar slipped piece by piece into her mouth during social studies.

When Andrew got to the special reading room, Miss Gilluly wasn't there. Instead there was this guy, a tall dude who looked like the pictures in Andrew's reader—white colored brown. He was wearing a loose, soft shirt and sand-colored pants.

"Hi," he said. "I'm Vic Watts. I'm a sp-p-peech

th-therapist. Who're you?" He leaned down toward Andrew.

Andrew put his harmonica safely into his back pocket and said quietly, "Andrew Blue."

"Ah—you *do* talk," said Vic Watts musingly. Then he asked, "Was th-that a harmonica, Andrew?"

Andrew nodded warily.

"What can you play?" asked the man. Andrew was surprised. He eyed Vic Watts suspiciously.

"Can you p-play something?" asked Vic Watts.

"Everything," said Andrew so softly that the Watts man had to bend down further. Andrew drew out his harmonica.

I can play everything, he played loud as a yell on his harmonica, hearing the words clear as day.

Vic Watts's mouth dropped open. "Great c-c-c-chords!" he exclaimed. "Can you p-p-p-play 'Old MacDonald'?"

No one ever asked Andrew to play anything. It startled him. He wished the Watts man had asked for something interesting—like Yolonda's CD *Rhapsody in Blue*, or his momma's *'Round Midnight*. But he attacked the simple riff of "Old MacDonald," playing it sharp and clean. Then he played it backward for fun. Then he stretched it into a reggae beat. He blew and stomped. *Eee-i, eee-i, oooohhhh!*

"Unbelievable!" cried Vic Watts. "You aw-aw-aw-ought to be at J-Juilliard. What're you doing here?"

Excitedly he strode over to the upright piano in the corner and grabbed some music from the stand. "Here," he said, thrusting it at Andrew. "Do you know wh-wh-what this is?"

Andrew looked at the sheets. He knew that these black marks were music, not words. This was music writing. Yolonda could read this stuff. He saw a pattern in the marks that seemed to make some kind of sense. He knew that the black marks told people what sounds to make. Some musicians couldn't hear the music in their heads. They had to read and play the sounds from other people's heads.

"This is 'Old MacDonald,'" said Vic Watts.

Andrew studied the notes more closely. They had a stiff, colorless look. It's not very good, he thought. Then he picked up his harmonica.

It's not very good, he played, clean and clear.

For a moment Vic Watts looked as though he might have understood Andrew. But then the eager interest left his face and the regular grown-up look came back. He took a deep breath.

"You don't like to t-t-talk much, do you?" said Vic Watts.

Andrew was puzzled. He wasn't sure what the Vic Watts man wanted from him. He knew what Miss Gilluly wanted. She wanted him to look at those reading marks until his head hurt. She wanted him to guess what the marks said so that she could say, "No, that's not right." And one time Stacey Goldstein cried when she guessed wrong three times in a row.

Mr. Watts had said, "Great chords." He had trembly speech. He listened when Andrew spoke through the harmonica. Andrew didn't think he understood it, though. What did "great chords" mean? Andrew wanted to tell Vic Watts, "No, that's not right." But he knew that could make a person feel bad. So he just played a little soft buzz for the speech teacher, trembly like his voice.

CHAPTER SIX

Stoney Buxton swiveled through a tight slalom course of his own design on Asphalt Hill. He'd set it up earlier, using pop cans for want of the slalom cones. Even though his skateboard was fitted with the wide, soft wheels more suited to freestyle tricks than speed, Stoney Buxton was still the fastest slalom racer at Willard School.

Stoney liked the howls of admiration from spectators, but mostly he liked the feeling—the twisting surfer movements, the melting swivel of his body as he eased around each obstacle. He loved the vibration of the board beneath his feet and he could tell by the sandpaper hum if his wheels were tuned for best performance.

As he whipped into the finish, he crouched, gripped either end of the board, and doubled up into a handstand. There was a spattering of enthusiastic applause from onlookers. And somewhere in the background, a peel of music—chords that echoed his astonishing trick.

"Hey!" yelled his friend Gerard as Stoney scooted to a stop and dropped to his feet. "Good move! You been practicing?"

Stoney's face was bright with sweat. He was black—blacker than black. Pure black. Hardly any black kids at Willard School had the dark of his smooth, inky skin. When he'd been working out hard on his board, his skin had the shine of rainy night streets.

He laughed at Gerard's question. "Nah," he said. "I just thought of it around the last cone. It just came to me. If I planned it, I probably couldn't do it." Stoney paused. "Where's the music coming from? I thought I heard some sounds skating right along with me. Not a boom box."

Gerard hiked his thumb toward a shade tree at one side of Asphalt Hill. Stoney had seen the little boy sitting there before. He was a thin, sweet-faced little black kid who always had a harmonica with him. Now he was joined by another kid, a blond second grader who sat a short distance away.

"Was that music *him*?" asked Stoney, surprised.

"Yeah; he comes here all the time. Messes around with that harmonica when no one's brought a blaster. Pain in the butt," commented Gerard.

Now that he thought about it, Stoney recalled sounds accompanying him often as he skated—not the heavy metal most skaters liked, but sounds that seemed to accent his skating rather than drive it. He'd unconsciously accepted them as part of the reward and thrill of his efforts.

"Maybe," he told Gerard, "but the kid is good. Maybe he'll add extra zip to the sport."

"Well," said Gerard, "this ain't no freakin' skating rink. Besides, the Dudes don't like him. He interferes."

The Dudes were what everyone called the junior-high pushers. Their leader was a slender, smooth-faced white boy in eighth grade. His name was Romulus Foster and he had the clean features of an Eagle Scout poster. He wore new and different jogging warm-ups every day and the latest tennis shoes. He was always accompanied by an oversized wrestler type, a black guy tagged Chimp, and a small ferret-faced white kid everyone called Leaky.

Rom joked a lot in a cool, confident manner and he was knowledgeable when he praised the performance of skaters. Even Stoney Buxton liked a good word from Rom Foster, but he refused the offer of Rom's little packets—even a free one. Gerard, on the other hand, hustled for praise like a nut-seeking squirrel in winter. Gerard lifted money from his mother's purse to buy crack from the Dudes.

"This stuff'll make me a star," he told Stoney, flapping a packet. "All the Hollywood people and athletes take it. Gives them more bounce to the ounce."

On the bank turns of Asphalt Hill, Gerard was nearly as good as Stoney. He was sometimes more daring and almost terrifying to watch. His control seemed last-minute and haphazard. Sometimes he didn't seem to know when to stop, couldn't unfocus from the trick or the slalom, but would keep on going until he fell down or wound down.

"I don't mess with my head," said Stoney. "And I like to hear the music."

"All that happy-crap music hurts business," said Gerard, nodding over at the Dudes, who stood leaning against some cars. "The Dudes get annoyed."

"Gimme a break," said Stoney. "How does a little kid interfere with those guys? He doesn't even look big enough for school."

"He cuts their action, I guess," said Gerard. "I

mean, I heard them bitchin' about it. Rom calls him the Pied Piper. The Pied Piper pollutes the hustle. He distracts. He upsets kids. Karl won't go near the Dudes now. The Pied Piper's made a wimp outa Karl."

Andrew, sitting under the tree, blew a few chords, testing the air. The two best skaters were talking to each other, and he was hoping to see at least one of them take off again. He had been making a special tune for the thin, black-black skater. His name was Stoney, and Andrew had invented a dancing sound for him, smooth and fast and happy. Gerard, the white boy who always wore a clean white shirt, had a way of skating that made you gasp. Twisting his mouth against the harmonica, Andrew had practiced a sound for Gerard—a terrified empty screech, like falling through air in a nightmare.

Now the older boys looked over at him, but they still didn't start skating. Andrew dropped the harmonica into his lap and listened some more. Yolonda hadn't come to get him yet. She was at the library or helping some teacher.

He could sense Karl getting restless where he sat a few feet away. Karl had told him that he didn't have a mother anymore. Andrew wondered what that would be like—not having anyone to worry about you crossing the street or worry about you finishing your food, no one to pick you up and dance around with you in her arms to music on the radio, not having anyone come home early from work when you were sick. Karl didn't even have a big sister, wonderful like Yolonda, to take him to the library and warn him about drug pushers. Karl had a baby-sitter after school until his dad came home. All she did was watch soaps and eat pretzels the whole afternoon. Karl said she never even noticed what time he got home.

Andrew lifted his harmonica to his mouth and played a few Karl notes. He played the soft wail of Karl's restless loneliness. Then he played a mother warning for Karl. Karl turned his face toward Andrew and smiled a small, relieved smile.

For Shirley's cake-baking lesson, Yolonda had finally chosen a chocolate fudge cake. There was plenty in the recipe for Shirley-whirley to do. She could chop nut meats, stir the chocolate melting over hot water, and grate orange rind to flavor the whipped cream. She could grease and flour the cake pan.

Yolonda's mouth juiced up just thinking about the different steps in making a chocolate fudge cake and spreading the whipped cream in thick whorls on top.

Although they wouldn't attempt the grand cake-making effort until after school on Friday, Yolonda had gotten stuff ready Friday morning before school. After their mother had left with her usual "Make sure Andrew eats his breakfast," Yolonda had carefully taken out her mother's crystal cake plate with its little crystal stand. She took the silver cake knife and server from their felt blankets and the pretty silver dessert forks, too. She set everything up properly on the polished table in the dining room, with her mother's best rose-flowered china plates and the pale-pink embroidered napkins used on special occasions. "Might just as well make use of this room besides walk through it to get to the television or answer the front door," Yolonda had said to herself.

The kitchen in Yolonda's new house was large, with wide windows overlooking the backyard and her mother's spring flowers. They had their own laundry room next to the kitchen, which meant that Yolonda could do the laundry. She liked doing it. Back home in Chicago her momma had never let Yolonda go alone into the basement of their building where the laundry room was. "Can't ever tell what kind of weirdo might have gotten in." Her momma had never gone down there alone herself, but always paired up with a neighbor to do the washing.

Cooking was more fun than doing the laundry. But it always seemed lonely working in the quiet of this new kitchen, no street noise enlivening the air. The afternoon that Shirley came to learn to bake a cake was the first time Yolonda was not bothered by the quiet outside their kitchen.

"Always turn the oven on before you begin—three hundred fifty degrees is what most cakes need." Yolonda showed Shirley how to set the oven.

"Now—first you have to sift the flour, then measure it, then sift it again." Yolonda used her teacher voice.

Shirley giggled hoarsely. "That seems excessive."

"It puts air in the flour so the cake will be light instead of heavy." Yolonda was wearing her mother's apron over her jeans and big sweatshirt. She had wrapped a dish towel around Shirley's skinny shape to protect her dress.

Yolonda measured and sifted into a big yellow bowl. Shirley admired.

"Then you soften the butter in the mixer." Yolonda set the mixer whirling, beaters biting into the hunks of butter, creaming it down. She began, gradually, to add a cup of sugar, using a rubber spatula to scrape and press the creaming mixture. It was tricky. Shirley admired.

Next Yolonda tipped the little bowl of melted chocolate while Shirley scraped it into the turning butter mixture. The chocolate swirled into the creaminess in a spiral. They watched the color of the batter change. The smell was heavenly.

"Now you can break the eggs in," said Yolonda. "Don't get any shell into the bowl."

"Yuck. Raw eggs are disgusting," complained Shirley. She tapped the first egg timidly against the side of the bowl.

"Harder," directed Yolonda.

Crack went the egg. Shirley screamed at the sight of the egg sliding out of the shell. The shell crunched in her grasp. It fell, following the egg, and disappeared into the circling vortex of batter.

"Great move!" growled Yolonda. She stopped the mixer and peered into the chocolaty thickness. Then she took a spoon and fished out the biggest pieces of shell. "The rest'll have to crunch up with the nuts," she said. "*I'll* put in the second egg."

Flour, vanilla, and the nuts were added. Shirley greased the oblong pan. Yolonda tipped the yellow bowl. The batter slid, slow as a glacier, into the pan. Shirley opened the oven door and Yolonda eased the cake inside.

"Whew!" she said. "Now we have to wait until it's done—thirty minutes at least." She set the timer on the oven.

"We're a pretty good team," said Shirley. "Good vibes. I bet we could really turn those ropes."

"Yeah, maybe," said Yolonda. But she pushed that possibility into a safe and distant future.

The girls went into the dining room to admire the place settings and the crystal cake plate on its stand. Shirley fingered the yellow roses on the dessert plates.

"My sister has a rose tattooed on her," she informed Yolonda. "They do it with an electric needle. She said it didn't hurt."

Yolonda was startled. "Why'd she do that?"

"For her guy," said Shirley knowingly. "She's a biker's girlfriend."

"Oh. It's like wearing perfume," mused Yolonda. "I myself prefer Giorgio to a tattoo."

"I've noticed you have this great smell," said Shirley. Then she asked, "For love or fashion?"

"For Tyrone," said Yolonda, and she began to tell Shirley about her great love, grown greater in the telling, for Tyrone of the flashing dark eyes and the funny wit . . . how he'd called her Londa.

"Is he back in Chicago?" asked Shirley.

"He's in jail," said Yolonda, pulling a sorrowful look. "He was my one true love and now he is no more." She sighed. Her mind avoided the deeper tragedy of Tyrone, his whole promising life slowed to a crawl. She skated on the surface of her sorrow, trying to impress this skinny girl with a dish towel across her dress. "My true and only love."

"Well," said Shirley, "I happen to know you love your little brother."

"That's not the same. Andrew's *family*," snorted Yolonda. She was disappointed. Shirley hadn't grasped the image.

"Where is your little brother?" asked Shirley. "I haven't seen him around at all."

Yolonda's heart stopped. Andrew! She'd forgotten all about Andrew. In her urgency to get things ready for the chocolate fudge cake, she'd forgotten all about her little brother.

CHAPTER SEVEN

The daylight lasted longer now in April, and it was late when the skaters at Asphalt Hill picked up their boards and headed for home. Only Gerard remained, joking around with the Dudes, his white shirt whiter in the gathering dusk. Finally, even he left, pushing off on his board. He passed Andrew sitting beneath his tree. Karl had left already. Andrew watched Gerard, one long leg working the board. At the asphalt's edge, Gerard tipped the board into an ollie, stepped off, and caught it. Then he loped across the grass, board under his arm, and disappeared down the street.

"Hey, kid!" The voice was friendly, even cheerful. Andrew, surprised, looked up from where he sat under the tree. Romulus Foster was strolling toward him, hands in the pockets of his new blue-and-silver warm-ups. He wore silver-laced Nike pump-ups with blue slashes that matched the blue in the jacket. Chimp lumbered behind him, followed by a scuttling Leaky. A trio. Something about their triple intent made Andrew stand up, despite the friendly tone of Rom's voice.

"You're pretty good on that mouth organ," said Rom. He stood with his blue-clad legs apart like an open scissors.

"Yeah, real good," sneered Leaky, who hovered behind Rom.

They lined up before Andrew, dwarfing him.

"Why don't you give us a tune?" said Rom.

Warnings went off in Andrew's head. He didn't like these guys, especially Romulus, who pretended to be someone nice. He would blow them away. He cupped the harmonica against his lips. He blew. He blew a sly sound—the fake Romulus Foster; he blew a snorty bully—Chimp; he blew a scuttle sound—the crablike Leaky. The sound gathered and sharpened itself, beveled itself into a sword or a bullet. *Fall down,* sang the harmonica. *Go away. Take a bath. Go away. Melt. Back off.* The music became a kind of spitting, a pushing. It prodded. It dug into Romulus Foster and slapped at Leaky and Chimp so that they leaned away.

Andrew stopped in midphrase. He turned and began to walk away. The three older boys were silent, stunned. It took Rom a full half minute to shake himself out of it. Then he said in a voice devoid of his earlier friendliness, "Stop him!"

Leaky scuttled after Andrew and grabbed his arm. Chimp plunged in and raked Andrew from Leaky's grasp. Andrew was too startled to cry out. He felt himself lifted from the ground, an arm like a vise about his chest. His feet dangled uselessly. Pressed against Chimp's damp T-shirted body, the cheesy odor of old sweat made Andrew gag. Someone was prying open his fingers, loosening the harmonica he gripped like a lifeline. Leaky squealed, "Got it! Got it, Rom."

Romulus leaned back on his heels, hands in his pocket. He smiled. "You need a better mouth organ," said Romulus. "We're going to take care of this one for you."

Chimp dropped the stunned Andrew to the ground.

"How we gonna do this, Chimp?" chortled Leaky. He tossed the harmonica back and forth between his hands.

"Lemme try it out," said Chimp. He grabbed Andrew's harmonica midair and dropped it onto the asphalt. He stared at it, sizing it up. Then he heaved himself up and came down with all his weight on the Marine Band harmonica.

Andrew heard the crunching clearly. He heard Leaky's cackling laugh. He heard the *umph* of Chimp's breath and the thud of his feet over and over. There was a final cracking scrape when Chimp took his heel and dug it against the metal and wood. The Marine Band harmonica lay flattened and crushed, wood slots broken in. Andrew looked for bleeding.

"Good thing," said Romulus Foster, smiling, "it wasn't your fingers." His voice softened. "I'd sure hate to see that happen. A friendly suggestion"— he paused gently—"keep away from the Hill. Go play on the swings."

Rom Foster turned and strolled off casually, followed by his two henchmen. Andrew sat for a long time where Chimp had dropped him. He kept his eyes on the mutilated Marine Band harmonica. He waited for everything to go away, for time to go back and for none of this to happen. He waited for his harmonica to become whole again. Then he heard his own ragged breathing. A broken cry scratched at his throat and it seemed to him that it came from the little heap of battered wood and metal where it lay on the asphalt.

*   *   *

"What's the matter, Londa?" asked Shirley. She followed the big girl into the kitchen. "What did I say?"

Yolonda's heart had frozen. Andrew! Had he been on the bus? She didn't remember seeing him. Asphalt Hill? Was that where he was? He'd always asked her before. Had he asked? She'd been so preoccupied with her cake-baking plans that she couldn't remember that either.

Her heart started up again. Now it raced.

"You stay here. Watch the cake. Take it out when the buzzer rings." Yolonda grabbed her jacket. "No. First test it with the cake tester. Hanging by the oven. Stick it into the cake. If it comes out with no wet cake sticking to it, the cake is done."

Yolonda jammed her arms into her jacket. "I gotta go back to the school. Just keep your eyes on the cake."

"Ahnnh . . . ," began Shirley-whirley, eyes jigging madly. But her voice was lost to Yolonda's back as Yolonda dashed out the door.

Yolonda tore down the steps and hurried up Fremont Street, her mind flying out ahead of her, crossing streets she hadn't even come to yet. "Oh Lord, please let him be okay." Answering herself, "What could happen to him? He's in this safe burg; nothing happens here. Andrew's okay."

Feet pounding, gobbling up the pavement, she

reviewed in her mind the dangers. Crossing the street. Andrew was dreamy, but he knew about looking both ways. Kidnapping. Kids were grabbed from safe towns all over America—especially pretty kids like her brother. Yolonda hurried on, sweat beginning to gather around her middle and under the hair on her forehead. Andrew was so little. He was so unafraid. But he was lucky. Maybe his luck was on him now. She heaved big breaths as she pounded on.

Then she heard Mr. Johnkoski's voice in her head talking about the drug pushers who hung around young kids. "Power brokers," he had called them. "They want power over other kids—like little Hitlers—like little Joe McCarthys. Fear makers." This town had its own version of Cool Breeze and his Hundred Gang. We might just as well have stayed in Chicago, thought Yolonda.

Suddenly, a stroke of intuition slid into her bones, making the perspiration chill on her body. The fear makers and Andrew. He always hung around the Hill watching the skateboarders. She began to run, big plodding strides, huffing, her jacket sliding back from her shoulders.

And then she spotted him. From the distance, several blocks away, the small figure of her little brother came slowly toward her. Her relief was so intense that it hurt. She stopped running and stood gasping for breath. She had a pain in her side and waited with her hand pressed there. But Andrew didn't dawdle as usual. He hurried toward his sister, both hands holding his harmonica. That was unusual, but Yolonda was too relieved to pay it any notice.

"Where *were* you?" she growled, more angry at her fear than at Andrew.

His eyes looked bigger than ever and so sad that they gentled her. Yolonda, never big on hugs, picked him up and held him close. She could feel his hands stiffen around his harmonica. He didn't smell right either. She'd give him a bath before dinner.

"I'm sorry I yelled, Andrew," she said softly against his hair. "Were you at the Hill? Next time make sure you tell me—and make sure I *hear*."

She put him down and straightened his jacket. Shirley was right. She sure did love Andrew. But now that the crisis was over, she could get back to Shirley and the cake.

When Yolonda held open the back door for Andrew, Shirley was in the kitchen cutting the cake into squares. But what a cake! Flat as a paperback.

"What happened to the chocolate fudge cake?" asked Yolonda, horrified. It looked like a big cookie.

"I don't know," wailed Shirley. "I kept opening the oven door every five minutes to check on it. It never got any bigger." Tears welled up behind the thick glasses. "But look, there's no cake on the cake tester." She held it up in miserable triumph. "That part worked okay."

"No wonder," said Yolonda. "Cakes won't rise if they keep getting a draft. Never open the door to look at a cake until it's mostly done."

She picked up a square and bit into it. It was warm and fudgy in her mouth.

"Mmm," she groaned happily. "It tastes great! Maybe we'll whip the cream after all." She offered a piece to Andrew, who shook his head.

Shirley took a piece, blew on it first, then tried it. "Fantastic, if I do say so. Doesn't need whipped cream."

"We could go into the dining room and use the china and napkins," suggested Yolonda. She nudged Andrew again with another piece.

"I like it here in the kitchen," said Shirley, munching away. "I like looking at your backyard and the flowers coming up."

"Maybe we've invented a great new recipe for brownies or something," said Yolonda as they sat at the table by the kitchen window. "We'll have to write it down. How many times did you say you opened the oven door?"

"About six times," said Shirley. "Do you suppose we should include a broken eggshell in the recipe?"

Andrew sat watching his sister and a girl named Shirley eat chunks of a big cookie-cake cut up in a pan. They took big bites and made *ummm* noises. The kitchen didn't seem to be the kitchen he knew; the yellow walls looked thin and see-through; light from the windows shimmered like running water. It was as if he sat and watched it all from another place like a stranger, not feeling the warmness, not hearing the girls' speech. There was no sound to play on his harmonica. He no longer felt the harp in his hands. He no longer felt his hands.

He slipped off his chair, harmonica hugged to his chest. He needed to do something. He wasn't sure what it was, but he wanted to be by himself.

"Come back and have a cookie, Andrew," hollered Yolonda after him.

"You mean a cake-cookie," said the deep man voice of the girl named Shirley. Their giggling followed Andrew up the stairs. A half-alive part of Andrew's brain noted and stored the mix of sound—Yolonda's giggle full of big bubbles, Shirley's coughing laugh like a car trying to start in winter. But Andrew's hands stayed closed as a coffin around the ruined Marine Band harmonica. He went into his room and lay down on his bed. He rested his burden against his chest.

Even his bed didn't seem real, nor his room. He was a stranger, like an alien from another world. He thought if he kept his hands closed in a certain way around the harmonica that it might stay together. It might get better.

Shadows grew long across the bed. He heard his mother's car come up the drive and stop. A door slammed. He knew in a far part of his mind that he would have to get up soon and come down for dinner. He couldn't seem to lift his body; it had grown so heavy. He wasn't aware of falling asleep.

Gradually voices crept into his sleeping. "Young lady! Your brother is upstairs asleep on his bed." His mother was hollering at Yolonda. "He's still wearing his jacket! Is that how you look after your little brother? And what was that sticky stuff I stepped in all over the kitchen floor?"

He heard Yolonda answering—the grown-up teacher voice—something about "nourishing friends."

Andrew drifted off again while he was thinking he would try to get up and take off his jacket.

He dreamed he was burying his broken harmonica in the backyard under the flowers.

*   *   *

71

Yolonda went to sleep right away despite the bubbles in her stomach from polishing off the rest of the chocolate fudge cookie-cake while she did her homework. She dropped off despite, too, a faint nagging worry that perched like a sleeping mosquito in her mind.

She woke in a flash in the middle of the night, the mosquito awake and buzzing.

Andrew! Something had not been right that afternoon, but she had been so relieved to find her little brother all in one piece that she'd been blinded to what her senses were telling her about him. She'd been in a hurry to get back to the fun she'd been having with Shirley, and the cake had been baking—so many things going on, she just hadn't paid attention.

He'd been holding his harmonica in such an odd way, and the look on his face—the look was one she remembered. From where? She couldn't put her finger on it. His eyes had been so big and blank. He had smelled sick, even. Yolonda gasped and sat up. "No!" She'd forgotten to give Andrew a bath.

He hadn't eaten anything at dinner. "Look, Andrew," their momma had urged. "Corn—your favorite—and applesauce. You like applesauce." Andrew had just sat listlessly at the table. Their momma had felt his forehead. "Feels okay—but you don't look right."

Yolonda couldn't get Andrew's face with its dead expression out of her mind. How could she have forgotten the bath?

He hadn't carried his harmonica to the table either, and that should have signaled Yolonda that he was not himself. Their momma had noticed. "Where's your mouth harp?" she had asked. "You haven't lost it, I hope. Your daddy gave you that. It's not a toy, Andrew."

Andrew had slid out of his chair and headed for the stairs. "Maybe you'd better go on and get into bed, Andrew," Momma had called to him. "You don't look right. I'll be up in a minute."

Now Yolonda scrambled out of bed, wiggled her nightgown down, and crept quietly to Andrew's room. She listened in the open doorway but didn't hear the sleep sigh of Andrew's breathing. She slipped quietly to his bed. It was strangely flat. Maybe he'd rolled out on the other side and would be sleeping tangled in his blanket on the floor. But he wasn't.

"Andrew." She said his name quietly, then in a loud whisper—an order for him to show himself. "Andrew!" No response. The curtain blew gently at the window. He wasn't in his room.

She hurried downstairs and padded quietly through the living room. The house was shadowy and silent. Sometimes Andrew came downstairs early in the morning and sat at Aunt Tiny's piano in the bay room off the dining room. He would sound a note or two with his fingers and just listen to it reverberate.

But now he wasn't there. Nor on the window seat in the dining room, another favorite spot.

The kitchen. He was coming in the kitchen door, a rustling shadow. He seemed so small, the light from the oven clock outlining his little-boy shape. Yolonda felt love and relief fill her, mingle together in an overwhelming surge.

"Where were you?" she demanded. "Where did you go?"

For what seemed like a long time, Andrew didn't say anything. He just stood there. An inexplicable sorrow washed through Yolonda. Something was wrong—bad—something was bad. She knelt down by his dark shape. His face was lost in shadow.

"Where'd you go, Drew-d-drew?" She used her baby name for him from long ago.

He leaned his head into her shoulder and she put her arms around him gently. His body was so slight.

"Outside," he said. "Outside to the flowers."

"What's wrong, Andrew? Don't you feel good?" She didn't ask him if anything had gone wrong yesterday afternoon after school. She didn't want to think about what might have happened to a forgotten Andrew while she was having fun with Shirley.

She carried him upstairs and sat him on the bathroom rug while she drew a nice, warm bath. She left out the bubbles. He seemed too sad for bubbles. He went willingly into the tub. She knelt and soaped him gently, humming in time to the washcloth. Then she dried him, bundled him in a towel, and carried him back to his room, where she found clean pajamas. As she tucked the covers around him, he turned his head and sent his gaze out the window. He lay that way, staring, as she backed from the room. "Night, Drew-de-drew. Sleep tight."

Back in her own bed she finally drifted to sleep, but shallow dreams pursued her. A devil danced. He lived, like the troll in "The Three Billy Goats Gruff," underneath Asphalt Hill and under the sidewalk where Chicago girls jumped double Dutch. Tyrone watched from a shadow wearing Andrew's eyes. She and Shirley were turning the ropes and the devil jumped in, his feet tapping "Pepper," his eyes rolling. Then someone cried out. Cried out. But not in her dream.

She woke up with the sound still in her ears. Then she heard her momma call Andrew. But their mother was never mad at Andrew. Maybe it was still a dream.

"Andrew. This minute—come down here!" Yolonda hurried out of bed.

"It's not a toy, Andrew," his mother had said. But Andrew had never thought the harmonica was a toy. It was part of him like his hands and his mouth, like his ears. It let him tell things. It was his power like muscles, like Yolonda's stare and her great big body. The harmonica was dead now and those bad boys—the drug boys—had broken it, and all the things that spoke through the harmonica, all the shapes and sounds that moved and waited and beat around him and through him and out of the harmonica were broken.

"Andrew. This minute—come down here!" He knew she'd found the harmonica buried beneath her tulips. It would take so long to explain it all to his momma—about the sounds everywhere, about the skaters on Asphalt Hill, about the danger, about lonely Karl and the bad big boys. He didn't want to make his momma have to "get outa this town," too. And Yolonda, who knew most everything about him, who always noticed if something might hurt him—she had gotten as busy as a grown-up. He had wanted to tell Yolonda about those boys—waited for her to help him say what was wrong. But she hadn't asked. Yolonda and his

76

momma both had said he didn't look right. But nobody had asked.

Andrew's mouth felt dry. Breathing shallowly, leaning into the wall of the stairwell, he descended to where his mother stood at the foot of the stairs. She was holding the broken harmonica, dirt smudging her hand. In his ears, replacing the usual dance of sounds, there was a hollow roar like some faraway water pouring down.

Shaking the fuzz of sleep from her head, Yolonda followed Andrew to the stairs. Her mother was standing at the bottom holding something in her hand. Yolonda watched her little brother descend, leaning into the wall. Her mother was never mad at Andrew, and she studied her mother's face. She saw the anger falter and dissolve, saw it replaced by a bewildered concern. Her mother opened her hand toward Andrew and Yolonda saw the Marine Band harmonica, broken and dirt-choked. Andrew seemed to shrink.

"Oh, Andrew," said her momma, sighing. "Andrew, I don't know . . . what am I going to do with you? You didn't have to hide your harmonica. I'm not mad."

"What'sa matter, Momma?" asked Yolonda, her voice still thick with sleep.

"Probably just as well," said her momma, ignoring her question. "The school has been complaining about the harp. Now maybe you will concentrate on relevant things."

"What's going on?" growled Yolonda, clearing the sleep away. "Is that Andrew's harmonica?"

"*Was* Andrew's harmonica," said her momma. "*Was* your daddy's, *was* Andrew's—now nobody's." She turned and headed for the kitchen. "Get dressed, Yolonda, Andrew. Breakfast." Her shoulders looked weighted down, and Yolonda heard another long sigh.

CHAPTER EIGHT

Why would a musical genius break his harmonica? Yolonda puzzled about this over and over. One of Andrew's teachers had even stopped Yolonda in the hallway at school. "Wh-what's the d-deal with Andrew's harmonica? The b-boy won't say."

Yolonda had just shrugged, her protective instincts flaring. Who was this guy anyway? "He has a flute at home," she had said, not lying—not telling the truth. There had been no waking-up music in the morning for days—ever since the harmonica-in-the-tulip-bed incident. Not a sound came from Andrew's little pipe.

Aunt Tiny had given Andrew the pipe when she started Yolonda on piano lessons. At first Yolonda thought maybe Andrew had broken his pipe, too. Maybe wrecking his harmonica was some kind of creative fit geniuses went into. Van Gogh painted ordinary things so that you could see them in waves of rippling color; he cut off his own ear in a rage of frustration, then painted a self-portrait with a bandaged head. She'd also heard of writers ripping up manuscripts they were unhappy with. But Andrew didn't get frustrated. He never judged his music. He just played it. One thing Yolonda knew: Andrew needed his harmonica. He wasn't the same Andrew without it.

"I don't think that's wise, Yolonda," her mother said one morning when Yolonda asked her for money to replace Andrew's harmonica. Yolonda was helping with breakfast partly because her momma had an early meeting to attend but mostly because Yolonda wanted money.

"If he's been that careless with a good instrument," continued her momma, "then he's not responsible enough yet to have another one." She whisked an egg into the buttermilk for pancakes. "Maybe it's a sign he's growing up. Miss Gilluly at the school has been disturbed by his hanging on to that old harp like it was a 'blankie' to suck his thumb with."

"Andrew never sucks his thumb," protested Yolonda.

"That's not the issue, Yolonda Mae." Her momma always stuck the *Mae* in there like a steel exclamation point when she wanted no argument. "The issue is that his harmonica has interfered with his concentration on schoolwork. Now turn on the griddle, please."

"Yeah, but Momma . . . ," stalled Yolonda.

"Discussion ended," said her mother, whipping off her apron.

Yolonda searched her brain for a way to tell her mother about Andrew being a genius, but her mother was in such a hurry. Yolonda couldn't get into the stuff about true genius rearranging old material. So she just got right to the point.

"Andrew's a genius, Mother." She used her teacher voice, serious and deliberate. "He's a musical genius. He needs gifted teachers who know how to teach geniuses. He ought to be studying horn or some other wind instrument. Did you ever listen to the way—"

"Have you turned on the griddle, miss?" Her mother was getting out plates. "Andrew is Andrew," she said. "He's a *normal* child." Yolonda thought she heard a flash of panic in her mother's voice. But maybe she imagined it. The panic flickered away as quickly as it had appeared. Her momma's voice was soft now. "Andrew is Andrew. That means a little boy, a pretty little boy. Your daddy's face must have looked like that when he was little. Eyes the color of chestnuts. Andrew is going to grow up to look like his daddy. He'll probably be a police officer like his father." Mrs. Blue paused, smiling. "Yolonda, remember your daddy—how fine he looked in his uniform? Tall, that broad chest? Remember? He always smelled so good."

But Yolonda was shocked into silence. A police officer? Andrew a cop? She was aghast. Before she could even get a proper protest or a sarcastic laugh out of her mouth, her mother was jerking into her coat. "Set the table right, Yolonda." Grabbing her briefcase. "Make sure Andrew eats." The door slammed.

Yolonda did remember her father's size. Andrew's fine looks and small-boned body were more like her momma's. *She* was her daddy's child, large and strong.

"The only one in this family suited to police work," she told her absent mother loudly, "is yours truly, Yolonda Mae!"

She tested the griddle with a sprinkle of cold water. It gave a satisfying hiss, a signal that usually made her mouth juice up. The weight of Andrew's genius forced her breath out in a huge sigh.

Today, she didn't even want her own breakfast, much less part of her brother's. She heard his soft step coming into the kitchen and she had a painful image of Andrew's extraordinary spirit sickening—all that new way of hearing ordinary old stuff growing dim. The guilt over neglecting Andrew while she baked a cake with Shirley surfaced in a rush and bit her. What could she do to take it back—to bring Andrew back?

First Yolonda had considered raiding Andrew's bank. After all, the harmonica was for him. Andrew got three dollars a week, which Yolonda changed into quarters for him. He dropped them, clink by lovely clink, into the slot of his giant panda bank. The bank had no other opening. Yolonda estimated Andrew had over a hundred and fifty dollars in quarters in that giant panda.

In the end Yolonda raided her own savings box and took eight dollars in bills and change. She thought she remembered her daddy saying you could get a top-grade mouth harp for about five dollars and Yolonda was allowing for inflation.

They probably don't even make the Marine Band harmonica anymore, she thought. But she'd look.

Her momma had said "no harmonica." But the stone-dead look of Andrew's face had been haunting Yolonda. She hadn't been able to get it through her momma's head about Andrew being a genius. Her momma wouldn't listen; served her right if her daughter didn't obey.

She waited for the bus to the big mall, her hand jammed against the money in her jeans pocket. They might just as well have stayed in Chicago where she knew how to take care of Andrew and herself, where she didn't need any friends. Where there was a bus every five minutes.

This bus took so long coming that she almost went home twice—walked halfway down the block. She almost never directly disobeyed her mother. She argued with her instead. She could hardly stand the feeling of being sneaky.

But the bus came and she climbed on, keeping Andrew's deadened face in her mind. Then it came to her in a flash who his stone-dead expression reminded her of. As she sat, her hands cramped and sweating around the crumpled dollar bills and quarters in her pocket, another face exchanged itself for Andrew's. Tyrone's!

She saw his eyes, their brightness gone. She saw the drooping mouth where once a sassy smile had caught her heart.

"Tyrone," she gasped aloud. Dragging through her memory was the image of his shrunken figure led away between two police officers. *Tyrone*.

What kind of prison was Andrew in? Yolonda felt her resolve strengthen. She would bring Andrew back.

The big mall had a lot of stores, both indoors and outside. It was Saturday and the whole area was filled with real shoppers and window-shoppers and teenage kids in clusters.

The harmonica in Kresge's was small—only four holes. It cost $2.98 and appeared to be fragile. Besides, it wasn't covered with plastic or anything. Any yo-yo could pick it up and slobber all over it. Andrew didn't need anybody's germs, and this harmonica didn't look like it would withstand boiling water.

Next she checked Toy Paradise, marching down aisles and aisles of towering warehouse shelves filled with toys.

"Harmonicas?" Yolonda punched out the question at a dazed-looking salesclerk. The girl, who didn't look much older than Yolonda, suggested aisle 22. "Music stuff is on the right, I think."

Yolonda found the harmonicas stacked between xylophones and an unserious mini set of drums. The harmonicas were boxed and wrapped in cellophane. They cost $4.98. "Two dollars for the box," thought Yolonda. The instrument looked exactly the same as the Kresge one—only four holes. Across the cellophane was stamped in red:

PLAYTIME HARMONICA FOR LITTLE MUSICIANS. Might as well boil the Kresge one, thought Yolonda, but she knew that neither harmonica could replace Andrew's old one. She hadn't realized what a good instrument her daddy had given her baby brother. Andrew had been able to get a wide range of notes on it.

It was a real music instrument, thought Yolonda, and then she realized where she had to go to find the right one. Andrew always watched for the Stellar Musical Instruments display window whenever they drove on Beckmore Drive. But it was a good mile-and-a-half walk from the Plaza Mall. She bought a couple of candy bars to help her get there.

Only half the journey had sidewalks. The juice of chewed caramel sluiced sweet and thick around her tongue. And then was gone. What a burg. Most people drove cars in Michigan. Buses didn't run that often, and Yolonda didn't know the schedules or the routes except from her house to the mall. She thought she would die from bored exhaustion walking all the way to Beckmore Drive.

The window at Stellar's held a gleaming set of drums, a bass viol, a portable keyboard, and a saxophone on a stand, all arranged as if musicians had just put them down and gone on a break. Yolonda pushed open the door and went in, suddenly energized.

Guitars galore were hung on walls. She'd never realized there were so many sizes and shapes and colors. A maze of keyboards and drum sets, music stands, horns on stands, and a giant tuba were arranged to divide the space into aisles.

"I want to look at your blues harps," said Yolonda, suddenly deciding that name had a more professional ring than *harmonica*.

"Any kind?" asked the salesclerk, an easy-faced guy with longish gray hair.

Yolonda waited. She didn't know what kind of harmonica, but she knew that waiting sometimes brought discomfort to other people and they would usually fill in the silence with some kind of helpful offering.

"How many reeds? You want twenty? You want a chromatic harp? What key?"

Well, she'd have to answer. "Ten holes," she said. "Key of C. Marine Band."

The man's face lit up. "One of the best basic mouth harps around," he said. "Hohner makes it, of course. Makes most of the good harps." He moved behind a counter in the middle of the store. "You said key of C, yes?"

Yolonda followed, smirking with success.

And there it was—the Marine Band harmonica, just like Andrew's old one, only shiny and unbattered. It came in a little black case with a velvet lining.

"How much?" asked Yolonda.

"This one's eighteen ninety-five."

Yolonda stifled an outcry by holding her breath. "How much without the case?"

"Oh, the case comes with it for free," said the man, smiling.

"Yeah, I bet," said Yolonda sourly. Then she added, "It's for my little brother who's a genius—a musical genius. Anything off for a genius?"

The man had stopped smiling. He looked surprised and amused at the same time. "Not ordinarily," he answered slowly, "but you bring him in sometime to blow me some sounds. I might take five bucks off."

Now it was Yolonda's turn to be surprised. "Yeah? You own this place or something?"

"Something like that," said the man. "Plus I like new sounds."

Yolonda sighed. "I'm not sure I can get my brother here. He's been acting funny ever since he broke his old harmonica. It was a Marine Band one just like this."

"Well, put some bread down on it," said the man. "Bring him in when he's got his stuff together."

"Hold it for eight," said Yolonda, digging into her pocket. "I've got to go home and get the rest." She dumped the money on the counter. "I'll need a receipt for this."

The salesclerk stared at the pile of money.

"It's all there," said Yolonda. "I counted it twice."

"Okay," said the man, and pulled a pen from his shirt pocket. He wrote, "Received on account: $8 toward Marine Band harmonica," and handed the paper to Yolonda.

"Add that there is only six dollars due," said Yolonda, pushing the paper back. She was nobody's fool. "You forgot that part."

"I wouldn't have forgotten that part," said the man. "But I want to hear the kid play. Don't *you* forget that part." He began to add to the receipt. He spoke while writing. "Eight dollars received; six dollars plus tax due upon recital by genius."

"Hurry up," Yolonda told him. "I gotta catch a bus."

After she left, she could feel the gray-haired man watching her through the wide window. She strode out into a power walk, strutting her stuff a little, showing off.

When Yolonda got home that Saturday afternoon, she found Andrew sitting at the piano alone in the house.

"Where's Momma?" asked Yolonda, sliding onto the seat next to him. Probably shopping, she thought.

"Shopping," said Andrew.

Yolonda placed her hands gently on the smooth keys. The piano was a power over which she had a questionable control. Since they'd left Chicago, without her Aunt Tiny's interest to inspire her, Yolonda hadn't practiced more than a few times.

"Your Aunt Tiny's piano's going to big waste, Yolonda," her mother was always saying. "Pity she insisted we take it. Tiny thought you'd practice, Yolonda. You could use those good hands of yours for more than pushing food into your mouth."

Yolonda, seated next to Andrew, reached up and opened the music. It was a Mozart sonata, fairly simple except for two horrible trills in the first movement, each a whole finger-lickin' measure long. She could ease into it. She flexed her fingers, shook the blood into her hands, flexed some more, and began to play, slowly letting her fingers press out the notes. She breathed easily like she'd been taught. The notes from the page began to slip into her mind and travel out through her fingers. She rarely had this experience. It was fine. Andrew leaned into her side so gently that her concentration didn't falter. She slowed down only a little for the horrible trills. At the end of the first movement, she stopped. Sighed. She put her arm around Andrew's small shoulders.

"Andrew," she said softly to the top of his head, "why'd you break your harmonica?"

She felt his body go stiff. She rubbed her fingers into his hair, making circles in his scalp the way she used to when he was a baby sitting in her lap. He began to cry.

The knowledge came slowly into her head.

"You didn't break your harmonica, did you?" she asked in relieved surprise. Things began to make sense. "Somebody else broke it." Her relief dwindled, replaced by a deeper guilt.

Andrew nodded, digging his head into her. Yolonda's mind groped through a series of possibilities. Then stopped.

"Asphalt Hill?" she asked.

Andrew nodded.

"Older kid?"

Andrew nodded.

"It wasn't your pal, Karl?"

Andrew shook his head furiously.

No, it wouldn't be Karl, she thought. Nor that Buxton guy.

"Gerard? The white-shirt kid?"

Andrew shook his head.

"The Dudes! It was one of the Dudes!"

Andrew kept very still.

"The Dudes, right? One of those junior-high no-goodniks?"

91

"Three Dudes," said Andrew, pulling away. He held up three fingers. He looked stricken and frustrated.

In her rising fury, Yolonda recognized that if he had his harmonica, Andrew would play their sound.

CHAPTER NINE

School had just let out, but the Dudes were already seated on the raised cement abutment that overlooked the deep, looping bowl of Asphalt Hill. A few skaters were arriving, boards tucked under their arms or hung by the trucks from bent fingers. Someone had brought a blaster that blared out heavy metal. There would be a steady stream of kids for the next hour.

On the abutment, Leaky perched nervously like an insect; Chimp hunkered down. Lounging in princely fashion, Romulus Foster sat with his legs over the abutment wall. He wore a handsome crinkly black jogging suit; his black-and-lime green tennis shoes dangled.

Yolonda could see them from the distance—no mistaking how they hovered over Asphalt Hill. Like vultures, she thought. She pressed Andrew's hand when she felt him balk and drag his feet.

"It's okay, Andrew. You can stay by the tree." Still she had to half drag him to his tree. "There's Karl," she said, letting go his hand. "Your friend is here."

Indeed Karl was there, on a flat part of the Hill. He was just pushing off on a board with a battered deck while Stoney Buxton watched. Was Buxton stealing Andrew's friend? She glared at Stoney Buxton out of her banked fury as she strode past, but Stoney didn't notice. "Don't watch your feet, Karl," she heard Stoney say.

The Dudes hadn't changed their positions on the abutment. Although her outrage toward them had mellowed through the school day, it began to charge up as Yolonda marched toward the trio. She knew Andrew was watching from there under his tree on the other side of the Hill. He needed to be there watching. It was *his* vengeance, part of her plan to bring him back to himself. But she didn't look back to check him. Her energy was gearing up. She began to hum tunelessly in time with her feet, her fists clenching and unclenching.

Her mind sized up the three older boys, strategy forming. Chimp, the stupidest, was the strongest physically.

She didn't pause when she got to the abutment but reached up in one quick motion and grabbed the dangling ankles of Romulus Foster. With one swift pull she yanked him off his seat. He landed with a cry of surprise and pain, his lean butt roundly thwacking against the asphalt.

Chimp grunted, rose to leap at her. She'd expected this, and when he jumped she moved into him and pushed him off balance while he was still in the air. *Nobody gonna mess with Yolonda unless they want their head busted.*

She caught him by the elbow as he fell. The elbow twisted away from his shoulder and he let out a bellow when he hit the ground. She held on. His arm bent away awkwardly behind his body. She pressed into it and he groaned.

"I got business with your friend here," she spit at him. "'Less you got some kind of weapon, other than your brain, you better stay put." She gave his elbow a final push away from her. Sweat was streaming down her face and beneath her shirt.

Leaky had jumped down from the wall and was circling her. She faced him, then gave a bitter laugh. She wiped her face with her sleeve.

"You gonna push me down?" She faked a move

toward him and he jerked back. "Get outa my way or I'll squash you like an ant."

She turned back to Rom, who was struggling to his feet. "Si'down!" She pushed him back down. Kept one hand pressing him back. His forehead clenched in pain.

"You don't mess with my brother, or you're messing with me." She pressed harder, leaned forward, and looked deep into his face. "You don't mess with my friends or my brother's friends either. You hear?"

She reached down and pulled Romulus Foster to his feet by the front of his crinkly black jacket. She drew him close to her, shaking her head so that the sweat would fly at him in big salty drops. She spoke into his reddening face.

"You broke my brother's harmonica. It cost thirty-five bucks. Got thirty-five bucks?" She let the question dangle like a noose.

Although she was victor for the moment, she knew she had to put up a shield for the future. So she lied some more—very quietly, very coldly. "I got friends. I got friends in Chicago. I got friends in and out of jail. Ever hear of Cool Breeze and his Hundred Gang? You are a small-time bimbo, and they are gonna kick your ass."

"Fat chance," gasped Romulus Foster with an attempt at bravado. But she could tell she'd gotten his attention. She dropped his jacket front. Romulus limped backward in a hurry.

"Fat chance, fatso," he said more boldly. He glanced briefly at Chimp, who had struggled to a sitting position and was holding his arm with his other hand. He shot a look at Leaky, who stood nearby, watching. Then louder: "I'd watch my step, fatso, if I were you. I'd watch out behind from now on."

"Yeah," agreed Leaky.

"Yeah, man," croaked Chimp.

"No problem, boys," said Yolonda. "My behind's just as big and dangerous as my front side." She turned in her queenly way and began to move, like a great ship through water, back to where Andrew watched, ashen-faced, from his tree. No one could tell, except Yolonda, that her whole body trembled.

Stoney Buxton had turned and was staring at her, his face delighted and surprised.

"You are somethin', girl," he said. "You are really somethin'."

"Yeah," said Yolonda. She didn't want to cut the power of her dramatic exit by stopping to hear more. She didn't want to slow her victory march. She didn't want Stoney to notice the trembling.

But she stopped. Stoney's eyes were bright with admiration. Different eyes than Tyrone's eyes—

mirth but not mischief. A hero deserves a reward, thought Yolonda. Maybe this is my reward. She noticed that all the activity at Asphalt Hill had paused. Only the music blared out, now useless. Karl was standing, one foot holding the board still. Nobody on the Hill moved. Her trembling began to fade.

"They been asking for it," she said, and then dropped her eyes demurely. "I had no choice." She wondered if the Giorgio was winning out over her sweat. "They messed with my little brother, who is a rare musical genius."

"Well," said Stoney seriously, "you may have just bought yourself a ton of trouble. They got friends."

"I got friends," said Yolonda again, reinforcing her lie, just in case Stoney was a spy. Just a precaution.

But Stoney was smiling. "I sure missed your brother these past few days. He really helps my concentration. Better than heavy metal." Yolonda saw his eyes flicker over her with something she hoped was fascination.

So she told him about the Dudes breaking Andrew's harmonica, "a rare antique inherited from our father." She wiped sweat daintily from her face with an old, creased tissue she dug out of her pocket.

Stoney looked over her shoulder. "They're leaving," he told her. "If you think you might have trouble with them, let me know. Two is better against three. B'sides, I can't let you show me up." And Stoney made a muscle with his lean right arm. It was the long, smooth muscle of an athlete.

Yolonda felt a smile broaden her face. She gave a delicate wave with her fingers and backed away, then turned at last toward her brother. She wasn't about to forget Andrew again, no matter how much fun she was having.

She could hear the activity of the Hill start up anew, the grind of wheels, the scuffing.

"Come on, Andrew," she announced when she got to his tree. "We're going to pay a visit to a man who's got this brand-new harmonica waiting for you." Now began the second part of her plan to reunite the loosened pieces of her brother.

Andrew was standing with the strangest expressions crossing and recrossing his face. Yolonda tried to gentle herself. Pay attention, she told the bold part of herself. Pay quiet attention to your brother. But time was wasting. She had a harder duty to perform.

This time she'd checked out the schedule of the bus that went down Beckmore Drive. There was one every hour. Time was growing short, and she was about to disobey her momma. The unfamiliar sneaky feeling crept through her. It was intensified by her earlier raid on Andrew's panda bank. All money means to Andrew is a pretty sound, she had told herself as the coins slid down the letter opener she had poked into the slot.

"Come on, Andrew. I got this planned just right." She leaned toward her brother. "Come on, Drew-de-drew, you gotta earn this mouth harp. It's not free."

Andrew wasn't sure where they were going. Yolonda had said something about a harmonica— not his dead one, the one that had the music in it, the one that sometimes spoke before he knew he had the thought. She wanted him to earn it. He was only a little worried. Yolonda never did anything to hurt him.

The bus ride was pretty long. Andrew was aware of Yolonda checking her watch and jiggling her leg impatiently. Every time the bus stopped to pick up a passenger, she let out an exasperated hiss. She was still perspiring, sweat running down her face.

Maybe she's still mad, thought Andrew. He'd never before seen the Yolonda he had just witnessed at Asphalt Hill—towering over those bad boys like Batman, bigger than Batman. He'd never seen her great power unleashed before, but he hadn't been surprised. He'd never doubted Yolonda could tackle anything. There wasn't anything she was afraid of. Some Yolonda sounds came into his head—great, powerful explosions. He'd need another instrument—drums maybe, a horn, both together. What instrument roared?

The bus stopped. Right in front of his favorite store. He checked the window with pleasure. There was a curled horn on a stand. Could the curled horn roar? He didn't think so.

Yolonda pushed open the wide glass doors. "Longhair might not be here, but I got a receipt somewhere." His sister fumbled in her jeans pocket.

Andrew stared at the wall lined with guitars, at the glass cases holding different kinds of pipes, bigger than his. There was a gigantic curved horn on a huge stand. Yolonda. Andrew was sure that horn could roar.

"Is this the genius?" A smiling man with gray hair that brushed his shoulders was leaning toward Andrew. Andrew scowled. There was that name again.

He could tell the man that his name was Andrew Blue, but his mouth was suddenly wishing for his old harmonica, the one he'd buried in the dark dirt of his mother's tulips, the dead harmonica. Where was it now?

Then he saw that the man was holding something out toward him.

"Where'd you get that?" asked Andrew, shocked and horrified.

There was his harmonica, only someone had fixed it up, polished it. The smiling man held it out toward him.

A sick feeling began to invade Andrew's stomach, and a faint hollow sound threatened his ears. Then it seemed as if all the instruments on the wall, on stands in the corners, inside the glass cases waited for him.

"All you gotta do to earn this baby is play something, Andrew." Yolonda eyed him. "Something great, that is. No chords. Play 'Round Midnight. Play Bart Simpson. Play the bacon."

Yolonda waited. The smiling man waited, holding out the harmonica. The other instruments waited. The hollow buzzing came into his ears.

"Andrew," said Yolonda in her impatient voice. "We got no time for games. The bus will leave. We aren't gonna wait another hour for the next one. I gotta dust before Momma gets home. You gotta play before we earn this harp. Come on, do your stuff."

The buzzing grew intense.

Yolonda grabbed the harmonica from the clerk, thrust it into Andrew's hands, and said, *"Play!"*

102

The harp in Andrew's hands felt stiff, wood and metal, no magic to it at all. No voice.

Yolonda's face grew more fierce. "Andrew! No more baby stuff. Come on!"

Andrew looked at the harmonica. He had no breath anymore, only a tiny little bit that sat in his throat, not enough to even whisper through the wooden holes. The air around him grew tight with everything waiting.

"I should have *killed* those guys!" exploded Yolonda. "They *really* robbed you, Andrew." She wheeled and headed for the door. "Give it back to the man. Get my eight bucks back. I'll try and hold the bus at the corner." She stomped toward the door. "I should have *killed!*"

Wait! cried Andrew's brain. Instinctively he lifted the harmonica to his mouth, felt with his lips and tongue the new wooden holes, felt with his hands the smoothness of metal, felt with his brain for the old voice living inside the wood and metal.

Wait! screamed the harmonica. *Wait! Help!* Yolonda froze, then turned slowly toward him.

Andrew wet the wood with his tongue, wept into the wooden holes; a crying spilled out of the Marine Band harmonica. Then jagged streaks of angry sound bled into the room.

"Whoooo!" cried the clerk. "Whoooo-eeee! Go for it, kid!"

Wait! yelled Andrew's harmonica. *Wait. Wait. Eee iiii eee iii oooh!*

"It's all yours, kid," said the clerk, clapping his hands. "You belong together." Then to Yolonda, "You owe me six bucks, sister."

Yolonda heaved a great sigh. "'Bout time," she grumbled.

Andrew looked at the harmonica while Yolonda counted out six dollars plus the sales tax from a great weight of quarters. His head felt like a balloon. It could float away maybe. He kept his eyes fastened to the Marine Band harmonica as if it were an anchor.

"Better take the case," said the man to Andrew. He held out a small black box. His smile was serious, and Andrew immediately trusted him. He could feel his head begin to come down to him again.

"What's it for?" Andrew asked.

"It'll protect your instrument—like a house around it—keep it from getting broken."

"Oh," said Andrew. His instrument. He took the case, opened it, and carefully placed the shiny Marine Band harmonica in its velvet bed. The lid snapped when he closed it. Safe.

On the bus as they headed home, Yolonda said, "Look, I don't have this all figured out yet, Andrew." She sighed.

Andrew waited.

"But you're *supposed* to have a harmonica. Maybe God decided it. Maybe your genes did the deciding. Maybe the stars. Who knows?" She chewed her knuckles.

"Maybe just Daddy," offered Andrew, who could barely recall a large shape hovering over him. He'd been told where the Marine Band harmonica came from.

"Yeah, maybe just Daddy," said Yolonda. "Momma doesn't know you are supposed to have a harmonica. I thought she did, but she doesn't. She loves you, but she doesn't see that you're a genius. That takes a rare mind—to detect genius."

The bus rumbled on and Andrew waited for what Yolonda would say next. He knew Yolonda was very smart. Apparently a genius was a good thing to be.

"I don't have this figured out yet, Andrew," repeated Yolonda. "Maybe you shouldn't play the harmonica at home when Momma's there. No, that's not right. Play it whenever you have to."

What did she mean? Did genius have something to do with secrets? Would he have to be brave? He held the Marine Band harmonica in its case gently in both hands. His instrument. In his head he heard the sound bravery made, but he was afraid to play it.

CHAPTER TEN

Aunt Tiny was coming! Oh, the glory of it! Yolonda helped her momma lug Tiny's special chair up from where it was stored in the basement. They had to push the love seat against the wall to make room. The chair was so huge that it made even Yolonda seem small when she sat in it.

With all the excitement of Tiny's coming visit, their momma didn't notice Andrew's harmonica at first. He didn't wear the new one in his back pocket all the time. Sometimes Yolonda heard him playing it in his room—just a bar or two of something. He carried it to the breakfast table in the morning in its case. Once, a week or so after its purchase, Andrew took it out and blew briefly into the warm kitchen a sound like the chair scraping when it was pushed back from the table. Yolonda stopped her spoon of cereal halfway to her mouth. Waited. But their momma was caught up in her morning flurry, and the harmonica didn't seem to register in her mind as she tore out the door.

That evening, though, as their momma was frying chicken at the stove, it must have worked into her brain—Andrew and the harmonica. She went straight to Yolonda where she sat doing her homework at the dining-room table.

"Where did Andrew get the harmonica? Yolonda Mae, answer me!" Yolonda had thought it all out beforehand. "A music-store guy, you know, at Stellar's—that big store. He heard Andrew play and he gave us a deal on the harmonica." After all, it was pretty much the truth.

Her momma's mouth dropped open with a faint pop. "Say what?"

"This guy really knows music." The truth, too. "He really thinks Andrew's a genius." Stretching the truth only a little. That's enough, Yolonda warned herself. Any more information come out, I might have to tell an out-and-out lie. Or the real whole truth. Her momma wasn't ready to take in the whole truth—about the Dudes and all. Who

107

knows what countrified place she'd want to move to next.

Yolonda's momma, hands planted on her hips, looked square at Yolonda. "How's that again?"

Yolonda calmed her face into innocence. "I took some money from my savings, Momma. And money from Panda-bank. I took Andrew to Stellar's. I thought the music store would cheer him up."

Her momma frowned.

"They had this harmonica there—a Marine Band. Just like Daddy's," Yolonda added slyly.

Her momma's face softened. "Well," she said, "I have missed Andrew playing his odd little music." She smiled. "Hope he takes better care of this one."

Yolonda took a deep, soundless breath. The crisis of disobeying had been averted, and she felt momentary relief.

But in the week that followed, her excitement about Aunt Tiny's visit was darkened by a bad feeling that hung over her like a poison cloud. She was not living up to her role as Andrew's protector, the brilliant young girl who could recognize genius. True, she had given the Dudes a pounding, and now, she noticed, they seemed to have moved their base to the park across the street. Yolonda knew they didn't want any more skirmishes calling attention to their activities.

Kids at school now eyed her with careful respect. Sometimes she could tell they discussed her in small, whispering groups. A couple of guys had elbowed her knowingly in the hallway, admiration half-concealed in their faces. "Way to go, Yolonda."

Yolonda had just nodded modestly. Her sixth sense told her not to brag. No good keeping things stirred up. No good pushing the Dudes into retribution. But driving off Romulus Foster and his henchmen hadn't done a whole lot for Andrew. She had failed her little brother. She had failed herself.

Although Andrew now had a harmonica, he didn't use it the way he'd used the old one. He kept it in the case most of the time, sometimes jammed into his pocket. When he did take it out of the case, his playing sounded tentative. Some mornings Yolonda would hear his waking-up song on the pipe, but it was not the same sweet, clear greeting. There was something ragged to the sound.

He's ruined, she caught herself thinking. Because of my not tending to business, Andrew has been ruined forever. She pushed the idea from her mind. How could a genius get ruined?

Aunt Tiny was someone she could tell about

Andrew being a genius—about true genius re-arranging old material so that it became new. Her aunt might know how to bring her brother back, make his music pure again. But should she tell about how she'd forgotten him for a whole afternoon? Tiny thought Yolonda was near to perfect. Would she be disappointed with her?

Aunt Tiny was a power. She owned three famous hairdressing salons in different parts of Chicago. They were called Trend and they specialized in elegant, time-consuming styling and classic cuts for African-American hair. Black women and men from all over Chicago and its suburbs flocked to her salons. "Goin' to get me a Tiny," they said. Beautiful hair models wearing Tiny's far-out hairstyles were featured in *Ebony* and *Mirabella* and *Vogue*. "Hair by Trend" said the ads. Even the opulent Oprah was rumored to have visited the main Trend salon on Michigan Avenue.

Aunt Tiny used to say she was a Black American businesswoman. Now she referred to herself as an "African-American entrepreneur." She always knew the latest style in clothes, hairdos, and the words to call yourself by. "Tell the truth," Aunt Tiny was fond of saying with her famous roll of her eyes. "I *set* a lot of the style. That's how I know it." And she would laugh her rich, buttery laugh, a sound good enough to eat.

"No," she had told Yolonda on the phone a month or so ago, "I don't want the piano back. It's yours to keep. I got a new one—a white one; big, grand. One of these days I'm gonna find time to play." Then her laughter had bubbled up. "First I gotta find time to *learn* to play."

Aunt Tiny could only play "Chopsticks." And a few jazz chords. But she had always owned a piano, Yolonda knew, even before she began to make lots of money. That's why Yolonda was given piano lessons. "Got this big machine in my apartment," Aunt Tiny had said years ago when Yolonda was only seven. "Somebody got to play it."

Yolonda had played it. She had taken lessons every other afternoon from an old man Aunt Tiny had hired.

For a while, back in Chicago, Yolonda had dreamed of becoming a great concert pianist. But her spirit didn't love the motion. She had become expert enough to play a little Mozart for Aunt Tiny. Mozart was the only classical composer Aunt Tiny knew and liked. She would listen to Mozart in between Stevie Rae Vaughn and Sarah Vaughan and Eubie Blake, complaining sadly, "They're all dead as Mozart now."

Yolonda's Mozart, these days, didn't sound like much. So she began to practice the piano frantically. She worked on the Mozart piece with the two horrible trills, trying for the ease she'd felt with Andrew sitting next to her weeks before. She also thought she might play entrance music when Aunt Tiny walked through the door, she wasn't sure what. Should she go with Momma and Andrew to meet the plane? Or stay home and prepare for the grand welcome?

One afternoon, Shirley came by, blue eyes jumping expectantly. Yolonda stood at the door, torn between getting back to the piano or maybe going to the playground with Shirley. Then she saw the old knotted clothesline Shirley had looped jauntily across one shoulder. That girl just wouldn't be discouraged.

"Where're you going? Mountain climbing?" Yolonda made her voice thick with sarcasm.

"Yeah," said Shirley. "I'm going to climb Mount Double Dutch. Wanta come?"

Pretty good, thought Yolonda. But she said, "No. I've got to practice the piano."

"Oh," said Shirley sadly. "Maybe tomorrow?"

"That's no double-Dutch rope anyhow, that raggedy thing. Mess your timing all up. You'll fall right off Mount Double Dutch, Miss Shirley-girley. Besides, I have to practice a whole lot."

Shirley paused. "I can get us a better rope."

"Have to be a whole lot better than that thing. And you need two ropes. Regulation size."

"Oh, I can get that," said Shirley. "Easy." She turned and walked back down the sidewalk, the old rope unwinding from her shoulder and dragging behind.

Yolonda felt suddenly deserted. Lonely.

"Wanta Coke?" she called after her.

"No," said Shirley. "See you tomorrow."

"Wait up," hollered Yolonda. She made herself walk slowly after Shirley, as if she didn't care all that much. "I do have to practice. My Aunt Tiny's coming next week on Friday and I have to play for her. Come on, have a Coke. I have some innermost thoughts to tell you."

"Yeah?" Shirley brightened. "Okay. What're friends for anyway?" She followed Yolonda, dropping the rope beside the door.

Yolonda popped the bottle caps from two cold Cokes and poured them fizzing over ice in two of her mother's good glasses. They sat at the kitchen table and Yolonda told the whole story about the Dudes and Andrew's harmonica. Shirley gasped and *oh*ed. When Yolonda dramatized her face-off with Romulus Foster, her friend clapped and squealed.

"Just don't mention it to anyone—how I whipped Foster's butt."

Shirley got very quiet.

"I'm trying to let it die down. Don't want to have to repeat my performance."

Shirley looked at Yolonda soberly. "I heard some gossip at school. Someone said you had a knife. Somebody else said you did karate you learned in Chicago. What you're saying's true, right?"

"Why would I lie?" said Yolonda—then caught herself. She *had* lied about double Dutch. She had told her mother near lies about Andrew's harmonica. "A knife is a stupid thing. Anyway, you can ask that Stoney Buxton guy." She looked into her Coke and poked the ice with her finger. "He saw the whole thing. He tells me to my face, he says, 'Girl, you are really something.'"

"Oh, no!" said Shirley. "What'd you say?"

There was time for a couple more Cokes while Yolonda told Shirley about Stoney Buxton and his good arm muscle and repeated everything he'd said to her plus a few things he hadn't said but she hoped he had been thinking. And then they talked about other boys in school—the cool ones and the nerds and the hateful ones. And, before they knew it, it was six o'clock and Yolonda's momma was driving into the garage. Yolonda hadn't gotten to the "innermost" part yet, the part about Andrew's dying genius. And she hadn't practiced the piano at all.

"I really have to practice tomorrow," she told Shirley at the door. "Aunt Tiny will be here next week. She's sort of famous. She knows Oprah Winfrey personally."

"Wow!" said Shirley. "I'd sure like to meet her."

"Maybe," said Yolonda casually. "It depends on our schedule. She'll probably want to do our hair 'n' all."

The admiration and hopeful envy on Shirley-whirley's face enlivened Yolonda. Watching her friend walk home dragging her raggedy rope, Yolonda told herself she would get up early to practice the piano before school.

Even though Yolonda's Aunt Tiny was really her father's sister, Yolonda's mother and Tiny acted like actual sisters. Still, Yolonda was sort of surprised when, the following week, her mother turned giddy with excitement. Yolonda hadn't thought too much about it before, but her mother didn't seem to have made many friends in this town—not any that she'd noticed anyway. Why, she's lonesome, thought Yolonda in surprise—a grown woman. The night before her aunt's arrival, Yolonda baked a cake and her momma decorated it with flowers and TINY spelled out in red frosting.

Yolonda decided to go to the airport to meet Aunt Tiny when she saw that her momma had filled the car with balloons.

"Won't Tiny be surprised?" her mother cried excitedly. She is acting like a kid, thought Yolonda, but the balloons had made her own choice easy. It would be so much fun to greet her aunt with a fistful of balloons.

"You and Andrew can carry most of them, and I'll hold a few, too," said her mother. "Tiny will love it."

In the lounge at the airport, they watched through a wall of windows as Aunt Tiny eased her great bulk out of the door of a small commuter plane and down the fragile-looking steps. How gloriously she filled the doorway as she entered the waiting room, bracelets jingling and scarves flowing in many shades of purple.

The great woman laughed her delicious laugh when she saw the balloons thumping delicately together in their bright bouquets. She took them all in one plump, beautifully manicured hand. From her finger winked a huge amethyst ring.

"They had to sit me in the three seats at the back o' that itty-bitty airplane," she bragged. Her face was as smooth and round as the balloons and perfectly made up. Yolonda hugged her, and she smelled as rich and warm as ever.

Then Yolonda pushed Andrew forward to enjoy the treat of Aunt Tiny's hug. Tiny pressed Andrew against her side and stroked the top of his perfect little head. Andrew's hand reached for his back pocket and stayed there, cupped around the new harmonica wedged in its case.

"Got to get me a bath, Josie," said Aunt Tiny to their momma. She fanned herself with the current copy of *Ebony*. Above her, the balloons danced slowly to the movement. "Will your tub fit me?"

"Oh, Tiny, you're a beautiful sight," said Yolonda's mother, hugging the great woman, too. "I hadn't realized how homesick I was till I saw you. You look wonderful!"

"Get me to that tub, Josie," said Aunt Tiny.

But they had to wait at the luggage-go-round for Tiny's bags. Andrew got to carry her red makeup case and Yolonda pulled her big, matching suitcase on its little back wheels. Aunt Tiny held the balloons delicately. They trailed out above her scarves like a part of her costume.

"Just look at my hair, Tiny," cried Yolonda's mother as they headed toward the car. "Nobody like you around here."

"Now there is, Josie honey," said Aunt Tiny. "Now you got the real thing. We'll fix you up to rave about."

Tiny stopped to rest, leaned on a car, then she bent her head as far down as her chins would allow and took in Yolonda.

"Taller," she said. "You're growing upwards, Yolonda. My niece is going to be tall as her daddy."

On the drive home, Yolonda and Andrew sat in the back with all the balloons. "What're we gonna do with these now?" Yolonda asked.

"Why not let 'em go?" said Aunt Tiny gesturing grandly toward the window. "Decorate the sky—more room there than in this car."

"Kills birds!" cried Yolonda and her momma at the same time. "Strangles them; the string does," added Momma. "We'll have to recycle. For now, they can float in Tiny's room."

"Well, it was a lovely surprise," said Aunt Tiny. She reached back and plunked one of the balloons.

Surrounded by the soft thuds and squeaks, Andrew thought he'd need his pipe to make the sound of balloons. Or the sound of their tangled, captive strings—or the flying sound of a bird.

When they got back home, Yolonda dashed from the car and was seated at the piano, playing, before Aunt Tiny had unwedged herself from the front seat.

Yolonda had decided on the Wagner bridal march. Da dum de dum.

She sang:

"She's never sometimey.
Her nails are red and shiney.
Here comes the fa-a-
A-a-mous Aunt Tiny."

Certainly her Aunt Tiny was never "sometimey," an expression Yolonda's mother used for a person who couldn't be counted on. Aunt Tiny could be counted on.

That evening was a real party. They feasted on crown roast of lamb filled with buttered baby peas, honey-roasted sweet potatoes, and their momma's famous orange salad with walnuts and poppy-seed dressing.

Andrew watched from inside himself. He didn't often see his momma so happy, laughing and lively.

At one point during the meal, his momma and Aunt Tiny began to sing at the same time. "Stop! In the name of love . . ."

Andrew marveled. His momma and Aunt Tiny pointed at each other, arms stretched across the table. From their open mouths, the song had poured out like escaping twin bubbles. "Stop! In the name of love, before you break my heart . . ."

Andrew slipped his harmonica out of the case and tickled their song with some chords. . . . *before you break my heart . . .*

His playing happened easily, the way it used to, but then he heard it. *Heard* it. The sound from his harmonica didn't go forward, spinning out of him, letting him send out another curl of sound in the old way. It stopped at an invisible wall and cut back at him like splintered ice. He choked on the sound, swallowing its coldness back into himself.

The wooden holes were dry and dead against his lips—were nothing but dead wooden holes. Holes.

Yolonda was looking at him strangely. She must know about the holes. Andrew dropped his head. Carefully he placed the harmonica into its velvet bed and carefully, carefully he closed the lid so that it didn't even snap.

Later, in the living room, they put on CDs. His momma opened a bottle of champagne—*thk-pop-ssss*—and he reached again for his back pocket, but only kept his hand curled there around the fat shape. They turned the music up. It was slow and hot. "Come Rain or Come Shine." Aunt Tiny stood in one spot and swayed to the music, then turned gently with small steps. She was wearing a brocaded robe of red and gold, put on after her bath. The robe streamed like a sunset, swirling as she moved. Then, with a sweet-breathed grunt, she reached and swooped Andrew up into her great soft arms and began to dance with him.

Andrew struggled. Aunt Tiny's embrace smothered all sound. I can do the music by myself, he wanted to say. I'm a big boy. He fought to keep from crying out.

Then Yolonda said, "Dance with me, Aunt Tiny."

Gratefully Andrew slid down to the floor and hurried over to the love seat against the wall.

His mother began to dance now, holding her long-stemmed glass of champagne and humming, watching her feet twinkle.

His sister faced Aunt Tiny. Yolonda's feet were light and she moved her body only from her knees. She wove herself around her solid knees like a Chinese lantern in a soft wind. Her head was high; she didn't watch her feet the way his momma did.

Andrew felt his heart grow full. A Yolonda sound simmered there. He drew out his harmonica and played the Yolonda sound. Deeper notes, they were, slipping in and out of "Come Rain or Come Shine."

Yolonda turned her face to him and smiled. Such a smile. What instrument could play that smile?

Then the music turned fast. Aunt Tiny sank into her chair with a gasp. His momma collapsed into another.

Yolonda danced alone. She flipped her heels saucily; her fingers flirted in the air. What instrument? What chorus of instruments could play his fabulous sister?

That night, in his bed, Andrew blew gently into his pipe, muted sounds—Yolonda's proud head on its strong, smooth neck. But that needed drums behind it. He thumped with his foot on the bedstead. Better. He played Yolonda's knees and the sway of her body over them. He tried playing Yolonda's smile, sweet and swelling wide open, on his little pipe. It wasn't working. He paused and thought.

Maybe his harmonica? Or both together. A violin? He'd never needed another instrument before. He wished for someone else to play with him and, right then, he knew he'd have to learn how to make the black marks of the music code so that someone else, too, could play the sounds he heard in his head.

CHAPTER ELEVEN

One of the great and terrifying things about Aunt Tiny was that if she didn't like your hair, she'd go after it. She cut JAZZ into the back of Andrew's hair and gave him a modified eraser-top.

She sat Yolonda in the kitchen and trimmed her thick mass of hair, working out of a red zippered case full of scissors and oils, curling irons and straightening irons. Yolonda sat on a stool with a sheet draped around her shoulders. She held a hand mirror so that she could check the progress every so often.

Aunt Tiny had just finished separating curly

strands all through Yolonda's thick hair and twisting each one with a fragrant oil when the doorbell rang. Yolonda's whole head was a gleaming mass of shining black corkscrews. She pranced proudly to answer the door, shaking her curls.

It was Shirley; she stared in astonished admiration. "Wow! Is that you, Londa? How'd you get your hair like that?"

"I told you," said Yolonda impatiently. Shirley could be so dumb. "My Aunt Tiny's here."

"It looks great!"

Yolonda tossed her head. The curls bounced and sprang.

"I can just imagine your hair jumping while we're turning ropes!"

Yolonda saw that Shirley wore a brand-new rope in loops over her shoulder. Lots of rope.

"I looked up the regulation size, Londa," said Shirley excitedly. "They have lots of good books on double Dutch at the library."

"No!" said Yolonda.

"No, what?"

"No ropes. No turning. No double Dutch. No *nuthin'*," she barked.

"But we were great at cake. We could be great at ropes. I feel it in my bones, Londa." Her gruff voice cracked to a hoarse whisper.

"My name's *Yo*londa. And the cake baking was

dumb. My brother got wasted while you were hopping around our oven."

"I didn't waste your brother, Yolonda," Shirley said, suddenly very serious, her eyes wide and flickering. "I was the one who reminded you he wasn't there."

"Are you telling me it was my fault?" An unreasonable rage suddenly flamed in Yolonda. "You think I let it happen? You think Andrew is ruined because of me?"

"I didn't say that. No, Yolonda. I never said that."

"Anyway, the cake was a stupid waste of time. Double Dutch ropes are even more stupid. And besides, no dumb-body here jumps good enough to practice for. I'm not wasting my time."

Shirley drooped, loops of rope sliding. But, doggedly, she continued, "You saying you don't want a friend? I thought we were going to be best friends."

"Best friends?" Yolonda bit the words, slicing them with scorn. "I got enough problems all by myself. I don't need a best friend, too."

"Everybody needs a best friend, Yolonda Blue. You, too. But it won't be me. It's certainly not going to be me." Shirley straightened her skinny little body and walked off the porch, pale hand holding the loops of rope against her shoulder.

Yolonda stood in the doorway, her rage dissolving about her. Well, she thought in miserable satisfaction, now I don't have any distractions. That Shirley girl was too much distraction. Still, the bad feeling grew even thicker.

Aunt Tiny looked at her curiously when she returned to the kitchen. "That a friend of yours, Yolonda?" she asked.

"She's a white girl," said Yolonda.

"Not what I asked," said Aunt Tiny. There was a pause, heavy in the quiet of the kitchen. Yolonda wiggled uncomfortably. She had to admit she hardly ever noticed anymore that Shirley was white. Sometimes she thought they might look ridiculous in public—Goliath and David, big and little—a great, queen-sized girl with a skimpy little toy poodle of a friend. But she didn't think "white girl."

"No," said Yolonda finally. "I don't have any friends in this burg."

"Too bad, honey," said Aunt Tiny. "You could have asked her in. You could have done her hair while I do your mother's."

For a brief moment, Yolonda considered running after Shirley. Catching her. Yolonda remembered her straight little body marching off. Apologize? Yolonda remembered the thin droop of Shirley's mouth, her sadly whirling eyes. I'd look like a fool, she thought.

"Thanks, but no thanks," she told her aunt. "I got to practice some Mozart."

But she didn't go in to the recently dusted piano. She leaned against the kitchen counter, watching, allowing herself to be drawn away from the bad feeling by her aunt's magical skill.

Tiny was doing what she called "a gorgeous number" on Yolonda's momma. She had unpinned the neat thick bun and brushed her momma's long hair into springy strands between her fingers. Then Aunt Tiny cut and straightened a slice of bangs across her mother's high, clear forehead so that one eye peeked out naughtily. She cut and layered one side short and perky, leaving the other side a bit longer. It made her mother look very flirty.

Yolonda was offended. Her momma was a mother and a businesswoman. She didn't flirt. She had *had* her day. What was she doing peeking out of bangs? How lonely was she?

Tiny didn't let Yolonda's momma look in the mirror as she combed and snipped. Momma's eyes were half closed in bliss. Yolonda was sure she would be upset or, at the very least, embarrassed when she woke up and saw how silly she looked.

Then Tiny wove layers of thin, glossy braids high up in the back and long, long down the back. Here and there, among the braids, she set little jet beads. More flirting.

Look at that hair, thought Yolonda, with those little beads winking away. She was mesmerized by the nimble movements of her aunt's fingers.

"Oh, Tiny," cried her mother when she was finally handed the mirror. She was not embarrassed at all. "Is that me? I'm *beautiful*!" She jumped up and hugged Aunt Tiny.

"Get me to my chair," said Aunt Tiny, wiping her face with a little embroidered handkerchief. "Girl, that's work."

At Trend salon, Tiny hardly ever did any of the customers' hair anymore. Only special customers. Stars. She hired the best hairdressers she could find to do everyone else and she just walked around making suggestions, chatting with folks, checking to see if they were pleased.

"Girl, that's work," she repeated. "Not many people can get me to work that hard anymore."

"We'll let Yolonda bake you another cake—one of her specialties, Tiny. What kind shall it be?" They had polished off the welcome cake the night before.

"Well," said Tiny. "That's good. We can eat it later. But you're looking so fine, we should hit the night spots this evening. First, maybe go out for dinner with the kids."

Yolonda liked eating at restaurants. But, disapprovingly, she watched her mother's excitement grow.

"I haven't been out in ages, Tiny. Not since Chicago. I can wear my black chiffon and my gold bracelets."

Yolonda sniffed. Probably lots of Giorgio, she thought grudgingly.

But when they tried to plan the evening, her mother's enthusiasm dwindled. There was no place to go in this town.

"There's a disco downtown, but most people wear jeans unless it's a holiday. Our only grand hotel has a rooftop restaurant, but"—here her momma giggled—"it overlooks the railroad yards and the Buick dealership. The food is gourmet frozen." She giggled some more, and Aunt Tiny joined her.

"Let's crash the country club," said Aunt Tiny. "You got a country club?"

"I look too fine for that place, too," said Yolonda's momma. "I look too good for anywhere. I need some elegance." She groaned unhappily.

"Elegance?" Yolonda snorted. "In this burg? This is a nowhere place." Yolonda began to feel better, superior. Everything was wrong with this place. Her bad luck had started here. She'd relaxed her guard here. In Chicago she could deal with stuff. She began to feel her Chicagoness, her fast-track sophistication. The inadequacies of this town made her sneer.

"You can't get roasted chestnuts on the street

corner," she scoffed. "You can't get a Dove Bar from a jingle wagon—just junk here." Yolonda was on a roll. She sensed Aunt Tiny on her side. "Kids listen to mostly dumb music in this burg. They don't do double Dutch with any kind of style."

Her homesickness overwhelmed her, blotting out the newfound favorite things: the good library; Mr. Johnkoski, the best teacher she'd ever had; Shirley, her newly lost friend; Stoney Buxton; and her victory over the Dudes.

Grimly she thought of the lost joys of living in Chicago: the busy streets, the gorgeous shops, great Lake Michigan with its giant hotels rimming the shoreline. The beaches, the boats. Grant Park with its flame flowers and roses. And the fountain there, the most sensational in the entire world. At night it was a spectacle of colored lights playing over palisades of lacy water. And, oh, the food! Cheap, too, if you knew where to go. No great food in this burg. And lots of nuthin'.

"And Momma, they've got drug pushers here too, just like in Chicago. . . ."

"*Not* like in Chicago, Yolonda Mae," said her momma, suddenly sobered. "In Chicago, a boy the size of Andrew would be bullied, his lunch grabbed, his tennis shoes stolen."

His harmonica broken, thought Yolonda, her appetite fading quickly.

But her momma continued. "In this town, you

can jog in the mornings without carrying mace or a billy club tucked in your belt. You can breathe the air here; your nostrils stay clean inside."

Aunt Tiny interrupted. "Josie, you're due a visit to your hometown. Why'n't you come back for the blues festival in June?"

Yolonda felt, for the first time in a long while, a leap of happiness and hope. "Oh, Momma, say yes, Momma."

"I don't know . . ." Her momma hedged.

"You need some Chicago-style nourishment, hon," pronounced Aunt Tiny. She laughed. "You need to breathe that fine, dirty air."

Yolonda's momma stood and walked to her garden window. "It's true," she said. "I'm starved for some fashion! I want to hit Neiman's spring sales. I want to walk through Saks Fifth Avenue. I want some Chicago pizza." She turned to Tiny. "I want breakfast outdoors on Rush Street Sunday morning with all those pretty people. I want to sit on the steps at the museum of art with the yuppies and hippies and art students. I want to feel that sweet envy of the Jaguars and the long limousines with their windows all dark."

Yolonda's momma paused. She looked at Yolonda. She said, "And then—I want to come back here."

When their momma was dressed for the big

evening she didn't look like their mother anymore. The black chiffon draped in soft layers from her small, neat waist. She wore a black satin belt with a sparkling buckle. Her hair flirted, the beads winking.

"No jeans, Yolonda Mae," she said. "You can wear pants if you like. How about those Mexican ones with the stripe down the side? And my big pirate shirt." Her momma was on a roll. "And get out Andrew's dress shirt. He'll wear his good pants."

Yolonda loved the pirate shirt with its great flowing sleeves and yoked back. Her momma let her wear it for special times. In the mirror she admired the large girl with the shiny corkscrew curls. She was adorable. She lifted her arms and the pirate sleeves fell in folds. The adorable girl smiled back.

Aunt Tiny draped a half-dozen scarves in red and gold over a vast, loose white dress. Her bracelets clinked and jingled. "Can't let all you beauties cut my grand entrance," she said.

Not to waste the splendor of how special they looked, they decided on dining at the hotel rooftop restaurant.

"You're safe with a steak or the lamb chops or the whitefish," Yolonda's momma told Tiny. She didn't even open the elegant tasseled menu.

"They'll be fresh. Forget the fancy. It'll be frozen."

Yolonda noticed that three men in handsome suits, dining at a nearby table, were looking admiringly at her momma and speaking in low voices. There had been a man on the elevator, too, who'd kept trying to catch her momma's eye. The maître d' had smiled hugely at her momma and kept on smiling at her while he seated them. He had come back to ask her if the table was "to your liking, madam." He came back again to whisk her napkin into her lap for her. Her mother was glowing, without even smiling.

The three men all paused in their eating to watch their table. The problem with being admired when you looked great was that people kept trying to horn in. And their momma looked the greatest. She wasn't even acting like their mother—or anyone Yolonda recognized. Their mother had become a beautiful stranger, leaving them all behind in her glory. Like Diana Ross, thought Yolonda.

Yolonda excused herself to go to the ladies' room. As she passed the table with the three men, she leaned toward them and said, "She's a mother. The one you're looking at. She's a mother and a businesswoman. She hardly ever looks like this."

Without waiting for a response from the three startled men, she walked sedately into the hallway where she'd seen the door marked POWDER ROOM.

In the powder room, Yolonda began to snicker, thinking of the surprise she'd given those men. She laughed out loud and it echoed, rebounding from cold pink tiles. "Wait'll I tell Shirley," she said aloud through giggles. How Shirley would laugh, too. Then she sobered suddenly. Shirley was probably not her friend anymore.

Yolonda washed her hands, soaping and soaping with a fragrant leaf of pink soap. She bounced her hair at the girl in the mirror. Her hair was a gorgeous number. "You stupid know-nuthin'," she growled at the girl who pouted back at her. "Who d'you think you are?"

All in all, it wasn't a bad evening. Through the window by their table, they watched rain come and the Amtrak train pass below them. On its way to Chicago, thought Yolonda. The lights from the town winked; the streets shone wet and black. The steaks were done perfectly and there was a big dessert cart to ponder over.

As they left the hotel, Yolonda thought, We're a pretty family—a pretty fine family. The doorman held the door wide.

CHAPTER TWELVE

Aunt Tiny would be leaving early tomorrow morning. There was only today, Sunday, for Yolonda to corner her—to talk to her about Andrew.

Already half the day had been spent on church and brunch at a lakeside restaurant. Another part of the day would probably have to be used playing Mozart for Aunt Tiny. Yolonda was worried she wouldn't be able to pull off the two horrible trills this time. Which should she try for first—Mozart or Andrew? She felt a rush and tumble inside herself, as though she were hurrying somewhere.

Her momma was busy in the kitchen, stuffing a

chicken for dinner. Andrew had wandered upstairs. Yolonda could hear his pipe sounding from his bedroom—the same phrase over and over. Aunt Tiny seemed to be napping in her big chair. When Yolonda tiptoed past, her aunt murmured, eyes closed, "'Bout time for some Mozart, you think, Yolonda?"

Time for the horrible trills. Aunt Tiny raised her chair to a more upright position. "I can hear you fine from here."

Yolonda knew she could see her, too, where she sat at the piano in the bay room. She stared at the keys. Here goes nuthin', she thought. Then, miraculously, she remembered to shake out her hands, letting the energy flow into her fingers. She played a few notes to limber up. "Just loosening up this machine," she told her aunt, hoping to make her laugh. No laugh. She could feel Tiny waiting. She began.

It wasn't easy. It wasn't hard. She stumbled a bit over the first horrible trill, but the next one felt right. When she stopped, Aunt Tiny applauded.

"You play real nice, Yolonda—a little tight in spots, maybe, but real nice to listen to. Don't have to be a genius to play so folks are pleasured with listening."

And there it was. The opening!

"I'm not the musical genius in this family, Aunt

Tiny," cried Yolonda, her voice yipping with eagerness. "Andrew's the genius in this family. You should hear."

Tiny laughed. "That itty-bitty boy child? A genius?" She smiled fondly at Yolonda. "Deuce, your daddy, used to brag that Andrew was the youngest harp man in history." She gazed off over Yolonda's head. "That baby boy was always tootling away in the background. Never really noticed him much—no bigger'n an M&M, that boy."

Then Yolonda told about Andrew playing the sounds of old west movies, and Homer Simpson, and how her brother could imitate the voices of newscasters on his harmonica. She told about Andrew playing the bacon and how he could capture car sounds and kids fighting outside their windows back in Chicago. She told about Andrew's waking-up music. She quoted John Hersey on true genius rearranging "old material in a way never seen before."

At that, Tiny said, "Well, I'm a bit of a genius myself then, I suppose. Family genes filtering on down." She smiled to herself. "That itty-bitty boy? I'd like to hear that song in the morning."

"That's just it, Aunt Tiny." Yolonda almost wept in earnestness. "He's stopped sounding great." And Yolonda told about Andrew and the Dudes and the broken harmonica and Andrew burying it. She didn't mention forgetting her brother while she had fun with Shirley.

"Sounds to me . . . ," said her aunt when Yolonda paused for breath, ". . . sounds like Andrew has got a lot to sort out. No way he's going to sound like he used to. Charlie Parker, you know, the great horn-playin' Bird himself, said, 'You can't play it unless you lived it.'"

Aunt Tiny leaned toward Yolonda. "I expect it's the same the other way round—if you've lived it, you got to play it. Andrew's waiting on his new sound, I expect."

Yolonda was disappointed. She'd thought that talking with Aunt Tiny would lift her burden. She wanted to ask her what to do next. She wanted to know how she could change things back. "I've messed up," she wanted to cry out. "I'm sometimey. I forgot Andrew. I've lied to Shirley about double Dutch." The words just wouldn't leave her mouth.

Tiny patted Yolonda's hand. "Don't get so down, Yolonda honey. It's not your fault."

It is! Yolonda wanted to cry. Another opportunity. She could confess now. But she held her breath.

"Andrew'll be all right. You'll see. We geniuses are good at hangin' in there." Tiny struggled to her feet. "How about a little piece of that cake?"

The opportunity had passed. Yolonda let out her breath. There was no way she was going to let her adored Aunt Tiny know how miserably she had failed her little brother. What was the point? She wasn't going to risk losing Aunt Tiny's admiration. It wasn't as if she were telling a lie.

By six o'clock Monday morning, Aunt Tiny was packed and ready to leave. She had rented a limousine and driver rather than fly back to Chicago. It would take her two and a half hours longer than flying, but she didn't think she could tolerate "that itty-bitty plane" again even for such a short flight. Yolonda was disappointed. She'd wanted to watch Tiny's plane take off, imagine her aunt settled across the three backseats like a pampered celebrity being chauffeured through the skies to Chicago.

Aunt Tiny gave Yolonda her wonderful fragrant hug. "Don't look so gloomy, Yolonda. You're coming back home in just a few weeks. We'll have us a grand time."

The limousine was big and luxurious. "Now this is more my style," said Tiny as the driver opened the door for her. Her smile through the window was big and luxurious, too. Then she was driven away.

The house seemed deserted without Tiny.

Yolonda picked up the breakfast dishes slowly, then had to rush with Andrew to the bus stop.

In school, Yolonda's hairstyle created a sensation. Heads turned in the hallway. Mr. Johnkoski said Yolonda looked "ravishing." Stoney Buxton stared in open-faced delight.

"Hey," he said. "Fine," he said.

Girls who had formerly paid her little attention now clustered around her, *oh*ed and *ah*ed and asked to touch the glossy, springy curls.

Only Shirley avoided her.

In the noisy cafeteria at lunchtime, Yolonda plopped down next to her at a table.

"I meant *best* friends," said Yolonda. "I meant I don't believe in *best* friends." Yolonda had begun to feel her horizons widen, her popularity expand. She was suddenly generous. "Want to come by after school?"

Shirley checked Yolonda warily. "I can't," she said.

"Oh, yeah? How come?"

Shirley's expression was difficult to read. "I'm grounded," she said, eyes flicking fiercely.

"No foolin'?" asked Yolonda. Admiration crept into her. "What'd you do?"

Shirley dropped her eyes, turned away. "I cut up my mother's new-bought clothesline."

"Well . . . ah," stalled Yolonda, startled. Well.

What? What a dingo. "That was a dumb move. I told you 'no way.' Didn't I say that?"

"You said regulation size. I looked it up. I got us regulation size."

That girl just wouldn't quit. Why was she pushing this rope-turning stuff? A flash of memory flickered in Yolonda—two girls in a Chicago school yard, hearts and minds joined. Something she could only envy.

Yolonda turned on her teacher voice, all authority and fact. "You need to be taller, bigger, stronger. Won't matter if the rope is regulation size. *You* aren't regulation size. How could we do ropes together? Besides, no offense, but I'm not sure a white person and a black person could pull it off doin' Dutch ropes. I'm not sure we would have the right vibes."

Shirley turned a reddening face to Yolonda, tight with frustration. "How can we have vibes," she whispered, "if you're such a bully? How can we have vibes if you don't want to?" Then her foggy voice rose, croaking angrily. "You're just making up excuses. So forget it! Let's just forget it!"

She grabbed at her backpack, dragged it past her tray of barely touched food, and fled.

Yolonda stared after her in surprise, shook her new curls, and looked around the lunchroom to see who might have witnessed the exchange. A few girls at the next table were staring, and Yolonda shrugged her big shoulders at them in mock helplessness and smiled.

They smiled back. When they returned to talking and eating, Yolonda sighed. Only now did she notice how empty she was feeling. She pulled Shirley's tray toward her and began to eat the remaining food—cold fries, the bitten-into hamburger. She drank the faintly warm milk.

Aunt Tiny's presence followed Andrew to school. Sitting at his little desk, he thought about how different his mother was around his aunt. Even Yolonda was different. She seemed smaller. She seemed quieter.

He thought about how they had danced that first evening of Tiny's visit, his mother giggling like the girls at school, Tiny's red-and-gold robe swaying with soft whishes, Yolonda's body rocking over the sliding lift of her feet. Not the harmonica sound, nor the pipe, could say Yolonda dancing. The big curled-up horn, he thought, might do it. He needed a round, big, sweet sound for Yolonda dancing.

Yolonda fighting? In his room, he had practiced on his harmonica a sound swift and sure as a shark attack.

He would have to learn the music writing. He liked the looks of it better than the word writing.

Some of the music marks were black feet, like Mickey Mouse shoes on stick legs; some shoes were see-through shoes; some had no legs at all. Mr. Watts knew about all those other instruments that could make the different sounds come. He had given Andrew music-word homework. He had told him about *A* for *Ahhh-cordian*.

That night Andrew found a picture of a violin in the newspaper and cut it out. He looked through the glossy pages of *Ebony* and found a picture of a bongo drum and a piano, too.

Next day he brought them to Vic Watts. Mr. Watts seemed delighted with the cutouts of the violin, the bongos, the piano.

"Let's talk bongos," he said. "Buh-buh-bon-gos."

Andrew watched as Mr. Watts drew a big capital *B* on the board.

"See the two drums?" he said, pointing to the half circles clamped to the stem of the *B*. "*B* is for *bongos*."

Andrew drew the *B* over and over again on the lined paper.

Bongos. There could be a bongo sound in Yolonda's dancing.

Andrew stopped making *B*'s. This wasn't the writing he needed. He needed the little feet writing—the little Mickey Mouse feet. He looked up at Vic Watts.

Vic Watts sat down, scrunching himself into one of the little chairs next to Andrew. His knees stuck up. Like a grasshopper's legs, thought Andrew. In his head he heard low notes creaking on his pipe.

"What's wrong, Andrew?" asked Vic Watts. "Don't you want to learn to write?" Andrew nodded eagerly. Vic Watts could show him. Mr. Watts reached for the workbook on the table, but Andrew put his hand over the teacher's long fingers.

"Not these," he said.

He got up from the little round table and walked confidently to the piano. He reached up and pulled down the music book. It was heavy. He carried it back against his stomach and placed it carefully on the little round table. Then he opened the book, letting the pages lie flat.

"These I need," he said. "I need the little-feet writing."

Vic Watts dropped his forehead into his hand. Andrew waited, worried a little. Vic Watts didn't seem to want to help.

"Which feet say the big drum beating?" asked Andrew. "Which feet tell the great big round horn to play?"

Vic Watts looked up and suddenly smiled at Andrew. "Sit down, Andrew," he said. Then he laughed. "The little feet won't tell you all you want to know. The other writing tells you if it's the drum or the tuba."

He unbent himself from the little chair and stretched up tall, reaching his arms high and groaning a happy groan. "Oh, Andrew, m'man," he said, "we have a lot to do. This is gonna take time, a lot of t-t-t-time. But I d-do b-believe I see the light."

He leaned down and rested his hand lightly on Andrew's shoulder. "Tomorrow, make sure you bring that harmonica."

Andrew smiled up into his teacher's face and patted his back pocket, like the clearest of words between the two of them.

CHAPTER THIRTEEN

Yolonda dozed lightly in the backseat. The comfortable drone of her mother's new used car made her feel safe. There was nothing much to do but read or nod in and out of sleep.

They were on their way to Chicago at last, and the excitement of packing and loading the car and running in and out for almost-forgotten things was behind them like an old dream.

Yolonda had tried to call Shirley to say good-bye. She had wanted to be able to say good-bye to someone. Shirley's mother had said that she was off to the playground with her double-Dutch rope—"my ruined clothesline" was how she said it. "She's paying double for the new one," Shirley's mother informed Yolonda with mean satisfaction. "Double for my trouble. That kid's just bought herself one hell of an expensive jump rope."

Yolonda had been startled that a parent would swear in front of a kid. Parents swore. Kids swore. But not in front of each other. Yolonda wondered if Shirley's mother was always so nasty.

Next Yolonda had wandered over to Asphalt Hill. Maybe Stoney would be there and she could say good-bye to him. He would grin, she thought, his intent, look-into-your-eyes, Stoney grin. And she would remember it all the way to Chicago.

But Stoney wasn't there. Just a few skaters she didn't know. Nobody to say good-bye to.

Would summer scatter everyone? She had just begun to get nods, even smiles, from kids. Would she have to start all over again in the fall?

Shirley still spoke to her and had nodded in the hallway, but her face was always closed up tight. Given a few more weeks, Yolonda thought, we might have started being friendly again. There hadn't been enough time for Yolonda to engineer that before school was over.

Yolonda grunted and sat up. Her mouth felt sour and gummy. She popped in a malt ball from the box in her jeans pocket. She felt itchy under her seat belt, so she unclicked it.

Andrew was asleep in his seat belt with his head against the window. The last week or so she had heard him playing on his harmonica a beautiful line of music, strong and pulsing. He played it, changed it, played it again. It had touched Yolonda inside her somewhere near the place where food was a joy and where she held Stoney's smile. Whenever she had heard Andrew working on this piece, she'd stopped what she was doing and listened.

Now he was holding his harmonica, fingers relaxed around it. The case had fallen to the floor. The smallness of his hands moved Yolonda.

He's getting better, she thought. Earlier, he'd been looking out the window and playing little chords.

Yolonda stretched and wiggled, bored with the backseat. Her momma relaxed when she was driving. She sang snatches of songs playing on the radio and her lips stayed in the shape of a hum as they droned down long stretches of road. Yolonda leaned forward, her ample arms cradling her head against the back of the front seat.

"Seat belt, Yolonda," admonished her mother mildly.

"I need to change positions," said Yolonda,

matching her mother's mildness. "Don't crash us just yet."

Her mother laughed. "Yolonda, you are so quick."

They rode in silence for a while. Yolonda basked in a vague peace. She played with some stray ends of her momma's hair, which still bore Tiny's glamorous cut but had been unbraided and unbeaded and was now rolled simply at the back of her neck again.

"Yolonda?" Yolonda steeled herself to resist the seat-belt command, but her momma asked instead, "Are you happy at your school in Grand River?"

Yolonda was startled at the question and couldn't think of an answer. She needed to know what was up. Why was her mother asking about school? Warily she asked back, "Why?"

"I've been thinking. You are such a smart girl. Maybe you need a special school. I mean, in Chicago, I couldn't afford a private school. But maybe in Grand River I could swing it. Your Aunt Tiny mentioned it. She'd like to contribute to your education, too."

Private school? Yolonda was stunned. She leaned back and buckled the seat belt automatically. Her mind whirled. *Give me time. Give me time to think.* Pros and cons. For some reason, she could only think of good things about her Grand River school. Mr. Johnkoski—definitely pro. She'd have him again next year. The kids? She was just beginning to break them in. Shirley—she didn't want to leave Shirley, even though things weren't so hot between them right now. Stoney Buxton. She could hunt him down in the fall if she stayed in the same school. Most important of all, who would protect Andrew if she were in another school? She couldn't come up with any good reasons for leaving her hick school—not unless they were moving back to Chicago. And even that would require some thinking about now.

"It's never too early to start thinking about a university," her momma continued. "Before we know it, you'll be in high school and you ought to know by then what you want to be. You can do better than I have. You could be the lawyer—not some assistant. You could be the judge, even. A doctor . . ."

"How much college does a police officer need?" asked Yolonda, for somewhere in the back of her mind she saw herself doing what her father had done.

"Police officer?" Her mother almost shrieked. The car swerved wildly for a brief moment and Yolonda was grateful for the seat belt. Andrew woke up with a little gasp.

Then suddenly, in Yolonda's mind, everything fell into place. Her mother just had it all backward.

"Momma! I've got it! The perfect solution. Andrew ought to have the private school, Momma. He needs—"

"Police officer! What's this about a police officer? Yolonda Mae? Where is your mind? What is in your head?"

Yolonda pulled back. She took a breath. She'd have to tackle this surprise panic of her mother's before she convinced her of the perfect solution.

"Well," said Yolonda slowly, thinking fast, "I could aim for chief of police as an ultimate goal."

"How did that ever enter your head?" her mother asked. Her voice was still sharp, but Yolonda could tell she was calming down—or maybe gathering her forces for an attack.

"I'm more like Daddy than Andrew, Momma. I'm big and I'm strong and nobody messes with me. Remember? You always said it."

Her momma sighed.

"Besides, Momma, I don't need a private school to get into college. I get straight A's now. I'm what Mr. Johnkoski calls a "prime candidate," a "first draft choice.""

Her momma sighed.

"It's Andrew who needs the special teaching,

Momma. I think he's an unrecognized genius."

"Oh, Yolonda." More sighs. "I know you love your little brother. And you're right. Andrew does need special help. For some reason, the school has him in speech therapy." Her mother's voice turned sharp again. "There's nothing wrong with Andrew's speech. He says words perfectly—not a lisp or a stammer. I've told the school I don't want this Watts character working with Andrew's speech. Next year, he'll go back to Miss Gilluly."

"*No!*" protested Andrew, struggling to sit forward in his seat belt.

"Ah." Their mother's voice dropped to a purr. "My sleepy boy is awake."

Andrew's face bore an unfamiliar twist of panic. "No!" he cried again. "Mr. Watts shows me *A*'s and *B*'s and *T* for *tuba*."

There was a silence filled with only the hum of the car.

Andrew looked desperately from his mother to Yolonda and back to his mother. "Mr. Watts shows me the little feet and how long they tap."

The car motor thrummed, suddenly very loud, it seemed to Yolonda.

As if to prove to them how much he knew, Andrew closed his eyes and said, "The Mickey Mouse feet go *tap*. When they dance in a row, there's a heartbeat in between. The see-through feet with no legs go *taaap, taaap*." Andrew's voice rose. "When Mickey waves a little flag, that tells you a quick sound—"

"That's enough, Andrew. What's gotten into you? That's enough silliness," said their mother. Then she muttered to Yolonda or to herself, "That's how they teach speech. They'll ruin my baby."

But Yolonda saw the frustration in Andrew's face. What was he talking about? she wondered. She had had no idea he even liked his teacher.

She put her arm around Andrew. "School's a long way away, Drew-de-drew," she murmured close to his head. "Momma will change her mind by then."

For the next hour, until they hit the outskirts of Chicago, Yolonda tried inventing ways to make that happen.

Then the shock of seeing the shabby approach to her home city sent Andrew's problem to the back of her mind.

Yolonda had only seen the Chicago that now greeted her along the expressway once before— when they left to move to Michigan. And that was at night from the backseat of their old car. There had been streetlights glowing and distant lights blinking all over the city. She had felt an aching sorrow at leaving all the beauty.

Now, amid heavy traffic in broad daylight, it

seemed fallin'-down shabby. Ugly buildings that looked as if they had been unpasted from one another lined the thruway. Paper trash was plastered against cement abutments and gathered with old leaves in corners.

Her mother hummed nervously and sometimes hissed when a car shot by, weaving in and out. "Idiot!" she fumed. "Idiot!"

Finally they exited from the thruway and dipped down and around and they spun, like entering the land of Oz, onto Lake Shore Drive. Here was the beautiful. Here was the Museum of Science and Industry and Soldier's Field. Here was the big birthday-cake dome of the planetarium at the edge of the lake and the gigantic Shedd Aquarium, like a luxury hotel for fish from everywhere in the world. Boats bobbed and dipped in Lake Michigan. Along the clean, long streets bordering the lake, joggers in bright clothes jogged; bikers in bright clothes biked.

Yolonda felt herself begin to beam with pleasure. "Look, Andrew, look!" she kept saying.

In the front seat, their mother chuckled happily. "Chicago," she said, and, without forethought, Yolonda and her momma began to sing it: "Chicago! Chicago! *Da-da*-de-*da*-da!" Andrew pulled out his harmonica and joined them.

Chicago! Chicago!

CHAPTER FOURTEEN

Aunt Tiny now lived in midtown Chicago near the historic Water Tower. It was a clean block with grand old apartment buildings. Elegant horse-drawn carriages waited for tourist customers at one end.

You had to be buzzed into the handsome lobby by calling Aunt Tiny's apartment from a phone in the outer foyer. The elevator was old, slow, and beautiful. Its walls were polished brass set with mirrored panels. The lighting was soft and golden. The door slid open noiselessly at the eleventh floor.

Tiny's apartment was huge, with vast ceilings and tall windows. You could look down at a pretty children's park and across at another big, old building. By one of the windows in the living room shone Tiny's new white piano. "I can play 'Frère Jacques' now," she joked. "Later on, Yolonda will have to give us a little concert."

"Maybe Andrew and I can work up something," said Yolonda, her mind clicking away.

Before they unpacked in the elegant guest room, she corralled Andrew and took him to the piano. She ran her fingers over the keys. They were light and responsive, with a silvery sound. Andrew was fascinated.

Yolonda began to finger out a Schubert piece from memory, making up bridges she had forgotten. And, in a moment, the sound of Andrew's little pipe was spilling around Schubert like sprinkles on ice cream. She was tempted to say to him, "Hold that till later. Remember it for Aunt Tiny and Momma."

She could hear her momma and Tiny giggling in Tiny's bedroom. Why couldn't they just shut up and get out here now while Andrew was doing his stuff? Yolonda worried that, later on, she wouldn't be able to capture the same easy mood that seemed to waken Andrew's gift.

She was right. That night, after a wonderful dinner of chicken and biscuits and seven-times-washed collards cooked with ham hocks, Tiny announced that it was time for Yolonda's concert.

In the living room, Tiny and her momma sat in what Tiny called her soiree chairs. They were pretty, with velvet seats, straight backs, and delicate curved legs. Tiny's own chair had been specially made in king-size to match the regular ones.

Yolonda sat at the piano and cleared her throat. "Stand there," she told Andrew, indicating the inward curve of the piano. Her hands were sweating and she couldn't get comfortable on the piano bench.

"What d'ya feel like playing?" she mouthed in a low growl at Andrew. Her mind was a blank. "Let's get this show on the road."

Andrew cocked his head and looked at Yolonda. He was frowning.

Yolonda could feel the heat gathering all over her body. Sweat moistened her forehead beneath her hair. The easy mood was nowhere to be found. Her momma and Aunt Tiny had begun to chat comfortably, no longer waiting. Schubert was out of the question. Yolonda needed a bomb, an explosion.

Suddenly her hands pounced on the keys and her brain sent chords from the middle of a Chopin prelude to the ends of her fingers. Left hand dug out the melody. Sound splashed into the room.

Tipsy. She hit a few wrong notes. Okay, though. It felt good. She played a few extra chords to steady herself. Awkward. She rumbled some low notes and then deserted Chopin completely, stabbing at the keys, gobs of sound erupting. She knew she sounded crazy. But Tiny and her momma had stopped chatting and were paying attention.

Then there was the rush of harmonica music like electric strands painted through the air, like a net beneath the piano noise—catching Yolonda's sounds, making them music. Wow!

She gentled, tiptoed back into Chopin, her right hand taking the melody, leveling off, fading away—soft now, melting into silence.

Yolonda dropped her hands to her lap. She turned to the startled faces of her momma and her aunt. "Just a little experiment," she said modestly.

There was a long silence. No applause. Then Yolonda's momma said, "Well, that's enough of that kind of experiment, Yolonda Mae. That was terrible noise."

Her momma didn't get it, hadn't even caught on to the soft, forgiving last part.

"I don't know, Josie," said Aunt Tiny. "I don't know whether they were playing new stuff—or just messin' around. Part of it made sense, kind of. You know, sometimes you can't tell, with this new stuff, if it's any good or not."

"It was a cacophony," said Yolonda. She felt superior and misunderstood.

"Don't you pull those big words on me, Yolonda Mae. I know noise when I hear it." Her momma shook her head. "All those piano lessons, and she wants to be a police officer."

Yolonda was relieved when her Aunt Tiny began to laugh. She looked at Andrew. His expression was satisfied and happy.

Next morning, Yolonda had no time to savor waking up in her beloved Chicago. Aunt Tiny woke her.

"My, my," she said, "this Chicago air must be too much for my big, strong niece. Wore you plumb out, looks like. It's nearly nine o'clock, and I've got an important job for you."

Over breakfast of biscuits and jam, Yolonda was enlisted to go down to Grant Park as soon as she finished eating to save them seats for the blues concert later that day.

"We'll never enjoy the music this evening if we don't have good seats," said Tiny. "Walk or take the bus, honey, but get us located in a choice spot."

"She can walk. She needs the exercise," said her momma. "And do *not* stray! Stay on Michigan Avenue." To Tiny, she said, "I have to remind myself she's only just turned eleven."

"Saturday is yuppie shopping day, Josie. Remember?" said Aunt Tiny. "Only thing you have to watch out for is pickpockets." Then she pulled a big, worn chenille bedspread out of her linen closet. With a sweep of her great arms, she ripped it in half.

"Here, take this," she told Yolonda. "I knew I saved it for a reason." She handed Yolonda half of the chenille bedspread and a bunch of safety pins. "No one gonna steal one half a chenille bedspread. Pin it on some good seats, baby."

It had rained in the night. Carrying the half a chenille bedspread over her arm, Yolonda walked the wet, familiar streets. Grant Park was about a mile away.

When she got there, workers were picking up trash where last night's concert had brought out the picnickers. The trash bins, sitting here and there across the flattened grass, were overflowing. Yolonda's tennis shoes squished as she made her way across the damp field toward the public seating area. It was surrounded by high steel fencing and wooden police barricades. She had to enter through a narrow entranceway. Chocolate malt balls kept up her energy.

The chairs were gray metal and hooked together in endless rows, a huge semicircle flanking the band shell, called the Petrillo Music Shell. There were already people there in some of the choice seats, saving whole sections for their friends. Some had brought umbrellas against the rain or sun—whichever came first. On the giant stage, a group of musicians was rehearsing, largely ignored by the early arrivers.

Yolonda chose the closest available row on the center aisle and spread the yellow chenille across the first five seats. Aunt Tiny needed an aisle seat and an extra one to spread out onto. Carefully Yolonda pinned the yellow chenille in several different places, hiding the pins in the folds. Anyone who wanted to steal half a bedspread, she thought, or steal their seats, would have to work for it. She counted the row—eleventh from the front. Eleventh row on the left center aisle. Good seats.

Then she wandered from the public seating area and up East Jackson to the corner. The stage entrance was there at the back of the band shell. There were lots of police everywhere. She found herself looking for her father among them the way she had done when she was little. There had been a family joke about how three-year-old Yolonda used to think every policeman was her father when she saw one from a bus window or when she was out walking with her momma. Even the white policemen. Her daddy used to tell that joke to everyone.

Now there were lots of women police. "I *could* be chief of police," she said to herself.

At the stage entrance some musicians were unloading instruments from a large van—a bass viol, a small keyboard, some tall African drums.

I should have brought Andrew, thought Yolonda. He would have loved to see this. *And they should meet Andrew!*

They should meet Andrew. Musicians at the blues festival were the great blues players of the entire world, coming to Chicago, where the blues were the very best. They would be interested in a boy like Andrew—a musical genius. Maybe someone like Sunnyland Slim, a mean blues piano man. He was old, with a voice like a dry wail, a bog-man voice centuries old that could get inside his listeners. Someone like Sunnyland Slim should hear Andrew. How could she engineer that?

The food stands were open already, so Yolonda stopped at the Japanese booth and bought herself a cardboard box of hot tempura to help her think. She crunched her way through strips of carrot, onion, and green pepper tangled together in their crisp puffed shells.

She crunched and thought. Maybe she could bring Andrew early tonight. She'd have to find the right musician. Someone who would listen to a kid. No one on dope. Dopeheads had no time for kids, no mind for kids.

Yolonda crunched and the tempura was gone.

She dropped the cardboard container into a now-empty trash bin. Tonight this bin would be over-flowing. The street would be too packed to move and there would be long lines in front of the food tents. She strolled up and down past all the lovely smells. She'd better load up while the getting was good. Maybe a rib sandwich now since she'd already had her vegetables.

CHAPTER FIFTEEN

Yolonda talked her momma and aunt into letting her out of the taxi with Andrew at the Grant Park corner. She said she wanted to show him the gardens of blooming roses. But she really wanted to walk by the backstage entrance of Petrillo Music Shell with her little brother. She hoped some musicians would be unloading their instruments.

"Wait till *after* the light," warned her momma. "Don't jump the gun. Do *not* cross until the traffic stops completely."

"Yes, Momma," said Yolonda wearily.

"And *no* food, Yolonda. Your Aunt Tiny has that

all taken care of. Save your money and your appetite."

"Yes, Momma," said Yolonda.

Cars were parked bumper to bumper along the miles of sidewalk. Long rows of portable toilet booths sat on either side of busy Columbus Drive. "Chicago's finest"— blue-uniformed police—were everywhere, directing traffic, sitting on horses or on three-wheeled motorcycles, standing about in chatting groups, eyes watchful.

Yolonda found that her technique for dealing with crowds returned with no trouble at all. Right shoulder forward, Andrew protected behind her big body—"Hold on to my shirt!"—Yolonda set a pace and marched ahead. She marched against the flow of movement so that people could see her coming. The crowd parted like the Red Sea.

There were no musicians unloading backstage at the band shell. Disappointed, Yolonda stood around, holding Andrew's hand. He watched the parade of people going by. Yolonda watched the hospitality tables that barred the backstage entrance like a prison gate. The banner above said MAYOR'S OFFICE OF SPECIAL EVENTS. A yellow-and-white striped awning shielded the tables where polite hospitality ladies checked the IDs of back-stage visitors. Nuthin' doing here. Waste of time.

Behind the tantalizing food tents marched Yolonda with Andrew. Steak tacos, barbecued ribs, roasted corn in burned and crackling husks—she could sort out each one by its odor.

They passed a washboard band zipping and clinking its music. Among them, a wasted, once-pretty girl, wearing a filthy yellow dress and a loose, vacant smile, slapped sound from a washboard hung around her neck. Her blond hair hung in lank, dirty strands.

"Acidhead," muttered Yolonda, wishing briefly for a camera. Most pictures of druggies were of black people. Andrew was gaping, but it was the washboard music that interested him, not the girl. She dragged him past. Right now they needed to get their hands stamped to enter the public seating area.

Yolonda managed to insert Andrew and herself in the middle of the long line thick with people waiting for hand stamps. It didn't matter that they already had their seats saved. You had to have your hand stamped BLUES.

Aunt Tiny and her momma were surely already seated. Tiny had smuggled in a hamper filled with food and cold drinks. Hampers and coolers were forbidden in the seating area. But Tiny always knew most of the security guards, usually Alpha fraternity brothers on summer vacation. She said they would never look under the big blanket and pillows she carried hiding the hamper.

Holding their stamped hands up so as not to smear the wet BLUES ink, Yolonda and Andrew looked for their seats. The public seating area seemed different jammed with people. Eleventh row, center aisle. Aunt Tiny was hard to miss, her great behind spread gloriously across two pillowed seats. Their momma sat up high, her neck craning around looking for her children. Tiny handed each of them a ham sandwich when they sat down. Their momma blew out a sigh and relaxed.

There was a group just coming onstage to do their stuff, young guys with zipper haircuts and a skinny girl singer in a red fringed dress, hoop earrings the size of her head. She held the mike and snapped her fingers as she sang. Yolonda ate her ham sandwich and longed for another. Checked Andrew's. He was still eating.

"How 'bout tuna salad, baby?" Aunt Tiny could read her mind. She was holding out a fat wrapped square and a fresh napkin.

When her appetite was curbed, Yolonda began to think about her plan to get Andrew next to the right blues musicians. The group onstage was too young. They couldn't know much or swing much weight. A *name* musician was what she needed— someone important, someone their momma and

Aunt Tiny would pay attention to. Someone to back up her ideas about a music coach or a special school for Andrew.

"Lemme see the program, Momma?"

"Please," said her mother.

"Yeah, please?"

Yolonda checked through the program carefully. Later in the evening, Fontella Bass would perform with the Oliver Sain Band. She was a name; so was Oliver Sain.

Yolonda returned the program, excused herself, and hurried out of the public seating area. Outside on East Jackson, the crowd had thinned some. She hurried up the street to the stage entrance behind Petrillo Music Shell.

Beneath the yellow-and-white awning, there were no black ladies guarding the performers' entrance. Just white ladies. Which one was more likely to let her get past? She studied them. White people were usually easier to con than black people. But these ladies didn't look as though they'd give an inch.

Yolonda sat on a bench to watch. A brass plaque set into the back of the bench said it was dedicated to Nat King Cole.

She watched reporters check in with the hospitality ladies. A guy delivering foil-covered trays was waved through. Food for the stars, thought

Yolonda. She kept her eyes peeled for openings. She had to get Andrew backstage where, somehow, an important musician would hear him play. First things first.

The whole area was tight with security guards wearing SWEET HOME CHICAGO T-shirts. Most of the security people were black men and women. No getting past them.

Maybe, thought Yolonda, I should hang around until Fontella Bass and Oliver Sain appear. But she felt a dull hopelessness come over her. She couldn't see any real opening.

Maybe later. Maybe tomorrow. Maybe nuthin'.

She bought herself an ear of roasted corn, holding it away from her so that the butter would drip on the ground as she ate. She finished it before heading back to her seat and carefully wiped from her face any traces of food. Good thing, too. When she got back to her seat, her momma's eyes raked across her face, up and down the front of her T-shirt, checking for crumbs, for mustard.

"Where have you been all this time, young lady?"

"Just wandering around," muttered Yolonda.

Her mother gave one of her sighs. "Well, sit and listen for a while. You can wander around back in Grand River. Here you got live blues to pay attention to." Yolonda sat.

The sun began to drop behind the great narrow buildings. Thousands of windows lit up, tall slices of yellow on every floor. The evening grew cool. Yolonda listened to Old Johnny Shines onstage, his drowned voice rising from Louisiana swamps. Grown-ups blew soap bubbles, iridescent spheres floating out over the crowd. Thousands and thousands of listeners cheered wildly after each song.

A pink moon came up in the pearly gray sky. Tall Taj Mahal came onstage with his red cap, country stance, and stubborn sway. He knocked out blues on his big guitar, diggin' earth, moaning out his song. The crowd moaned. Swayed.

A chubby woman, black as coffee beans, danced drunkenly in the aisles. Security guards warned her to settle down. She ignored them, chin stubborn, arms waving. Her blouse kept riding up and a little roll of fat would spill out over her pants. Once she fell down. After that she really got going, high-stepping, hips swimming through the air. The guards, one on each side, took her away up the aisle, still dancing, stepping on their feet.

Night insects swam in the corridors of light sent from great spotlights onto the stage. And the blues spilled from the musicians.

Onstage with a lively group, John Hammond, a handsome white guy, had looked placid as an underwear manikin. Then he began to sing, his guitar across his lap, harmonica attached to his collar. "Oh, you may bare my body—my bodeeeah . . ." Wow, lotta heat, thought Yolonda. Lotta heat for someone looking straight and chilly as a snow cone.

Yolonda began to imagine Andrew onstage playing his harmonica. Maybe she could accompany him on the piano. The audience would scream and clap wildly.

The sky grew dark blue behind the moon that was now yellow as an egg yolk. Then on came Fontella Bass and Oliver Sain, and they pulled Yolonda into the excitement swelling through the listening crowd.

Fontella Bass was wearing a white dress fringed all around below her hips, the skirt so narrow it hugged her walk into tiny doll steps beneath her big, shapely form. "No matter, no matter, no matter, no matter," she wailed, "no matter what you do . . ." The fringe on her dress swayed against her broad movements.

Oliver Sain pulled sound through a saxophone like a magician pulling a handkerchief through a ring. "Ain't no sunshine when I'm blue . . . ," sang Fontella Bass.

And the crowd went crazy when she finished. Even Aunt Tiny rose, chanting, to her feet. "Do it, girl. Do it!" Standing and stomping, clapping and whistling, sixty thousand people begged for more.

The MC wore a straw hat and a vest over a little pot of a stomach. "Is this the finest blues in the world? Let's hear it, Chicago! Is this the finest blues city in the world? You know what I'm talking about this evening? You know? You know?"

The crowd whistled, cried out. "Yeah, yeah! Awright! Woo! Git down!" They went nuts, waving hands, leaping up, dancing in the aisles. Police and security guards grew grim faces. "Yeah, yeah, yea-ah!"

They'll never come back on and play some more, thought Yolonda with disappointment as Fontella Bass and Oliver Sain came back only to bow again. They are escaping right now. And I'll never reach them with Andrew anyway, so what's the point? But at that moment, something happened onstage that set Yolonda's mind whirling.

The MC cried out, "While I have your attention . . ." Much laughter at this. "While I have your indulgence . . ."

A backstage assistant came forward carrying a tiny little boy. He handed him to the announcer. The boy, maybe three years old, had blond wispy curls and he was weeping.

"We've got a little lost boy here. Momma and Poppa? You out there?"

The entire crowd went silent. Then, as if from one heart, they sighed and cooed. "Ooooooooh!"

cooed the crowd. "Aaaaaaaaw!" sighed the crowd.

The little blond boy stopped crying and wiped his hand through his hair. Cocked his head. Looked at the crowd.

"Aaaaaaaaw!" sighed the crowd.

Look at that dumb little kid, thought Yolonda. Didn't do nuthin' to get all that recognition but get himself lost.

And there it was. The plan.

It simmered and bubbled inside Yolonda. Her spirits lifted. Her heart began to race. A plan had come to her at last.

CHAPTER SIXTEEN

Yolonda had always loved the softness of Sunday morning sounds in Chicago, the absence of traffic bustle. But she couldn't hear much of anything from Tiny's high apartment when she woke the next morning—even with the windows open. She leaned her head from the window. The little park below was empty except for an old man on a bench. The day was blossoming, cool and bright.

"We're gonna need jackets in Grant Park this evening," sang Aunt Tiny from her dressing room. "You know—that wind off the lake."

Yolonda decided to go down to Grant Park a little earlier to save the seats. She'd have an even better pick of spots. Besides, she needed to case the grounds.

"I'm off to pin the seats," she hollered to Tiny—to her mother—whoever was listening. She grabbed a granola bar to munch on the way.

The public seating area was almost empty—just a few rows were marked out with paper bags over backs of chairs or tape running along the seats. She pinned the yellow chenille half bedspread across five seats on the same center aisle but in the sixth row this time.

She bought red beans and rice with Louisiana sausage at the Bayou food tent. Breakfast. She sat on the Nat King Cole bench to work out her moves for the big plan. She ate slowly, savoring the mealy mash of beans and rice in her mouth, biting off chunks of the sausage she speared with the silly plastic fork.

Now that she had a basic plan, things she observed fell right into place like water into a waiting bucket. There were only a few ladies under the yellow-and-white awning this early. They were casual and chatty, drinking coffee from plastic cups and nibbling Danish. Two of them were well-dressed black women. They all seemed easy and pleasant now in the light of Yolonda's plan—even helpful—no longer the fierce protectors of big-time musicians.

From her jacket pocket, Yolonda pulled out the folded program.

Tonight on the big stage of Petrillo Music Shell there would be some blues big-timers she recognized and some she didn't. Koko Taylor, Yolonda remembered, could drive the blues right through your body with her big voice and her gold teeth flashing. Little Willie Littlefield was on the program, and someone named Davie Rae Shawn. The great B. B. King would wind up the evening.

Yolonda imagined that backstage before their performances big-time musicians chatted with one another, admired one another's costumes, exchanged trade gossip, sat in flower-filled dressing rooms on comfortable couches. They nibbled on whatever treats were brought in on foil-covered trays. Maybe they drank champagne back there. They would be relaxed, waiting until someone knocked on the door and said something like, "Five minutes, Ms. Taylor. Five minutes, Mr. King." Then the big-time musicians would toss down the last of the champagne from their fluted glasses, pick up their instruments, smooth down their sequins, and sweep onto the stage.

Sometime, somehow, during that relaxed time was when they must discover Andrew Blue. It had to appear to be an accident. First things first. First get past the yellow-striped awnings into the inner sanctum. The big plan would do that.

Yolonda needed to know where lost kids went when they were lost. If kids were lost, they didn't know anything, least of all where to go to get found. Then what did they do? They probably cried until someone noticed.

Yolonda remembered the unified sympathy of sixty thousand people when the tiny blond-haired boy had been brought onstage. *Aaaaaaaw.*

Maybe lost kids just stood and called, "Momma. Momma!" over and over. Something Andrew would never do even if he were lost. Yolonda sighed. There were some hitches in her big plan. She'd better get started.

She finished her beans and rice, dumped the plate and fork into a trash bin. Surveying the ladies under the awning, she chose a short blond, the one who seemed to be doing the most talking.

"Excuse me," she said in her intelligent-but-modest voice.

The talkative lady turned.

"Where would a lost child go to get found?"

A smile lit up the lady's face. Good choice, thought Yolonda. This woman was a people helper.

"Any police officer can help, dear. Are you looking for a lost child?"

"No, uh . . ." Yolonda stalled. Her brain flashed

and sifted through a number of answers until she came to the right one. "No, just want to know what to tell my little brother."

The helpful lady nodded. Maybe she'd had a little brother once. But the other ladies looked at Yolonda none too warmly. One of them had narrow eyes that regarded her with mistrust.

Yolonda lifted her head gracefully and said in her superior voice, "In the event that he strays— this evening—when the crowd becomes impérmeable." She let the last word hang in the air.

The narrow-eyed woman tilted her head in surprise, and then her face sort of caved in. "Make sure he knows how to spell his last name, young lady," she said. "And knows his address—including zip code."

Inside Yolonda grinned. Outside she kept her face closed and cool. "How can you tell when a child is really lost?" she asked. "I mean if he doesn't say anything."

"Oh," laughed one of the women, "you can most always spot them. They have desolate faces. They keep looking around."

"And they clutch whatever they're carrying," offered another woman.

"Their eyes all huge. They look terrified."

All the women were helping now, even one sitting at a table by the entrance.

"Lots of times they don't cry until you ask them if they've lost their mother. Then it's Niagara Falls."

The talkative woman said, "There's a temporary police post right across the street—right under the trees there." She pointed past the beer tent at the end of the block. "Lost children are taken there."

Not onto the stage?

"Wouldn't they bring him out on the stage?" asked Yolonda, her plan teetering in her head.

All the women stared at her.

"He's so little. It might scare him."

"No," snapped the narrow-eyed woman. "No, that's a last resort. If nobody comes in a couple of hours to claim the lost child, then they might bring it onstage." The woman smiled a tight, satisfied smile at Yolonda.

Yolonda used her polite, cool voice: "Thank you very much," and turned to leave. "This is very helpful information." She gave them all a short smile and a short wave.

She headed up the street, shaking off the eyes of the hospitality ladies, which she was sure were fastened to her back. There were fourteen long blocks back to Tiny's apartment house, but Yolonda resisted the urge to stop at Fanny Mae's for an ice-cream bar to accompany her long walk. She wanted to get back in time to talk Aunt Tiny into doing a quick number on her hair.

That afternoon, she took more care than usual with dressing, selecting a jumper and a lace-collared blouse instead of blue jeans and her favorite yellow T-shirt. She was glad now that her momma had made her bring the jumper. "It makes you look more your age, not like some teenager."

Tiny had given Yolonda a frame of springy curls around her face and pulled the rest of her hair back into a thick braid. The braid was good. Yolonda thought it helped make her appear even younger. Looking into the mirror, she made her eyes go big. She tried for innocence. She tried for terror. She tried looking helpless like a lost child would look. Helpless was impossible; she only looked gooey. Terror was pretty good, but Yolonda didn't want to give the impression that someone was after her. She tried for a mixture of innocence and terror. The hair helped with the innocence.

Usually Andrew left his pipe at home when he went out anywhere, but on this Sunday he was surprised when Yolonda tied it around his neck with a thin ribbon. "Why don't you let me carry the Marine Band case?" she suggested. She was wearing a skirt, he noticed. It had big pockets. "That way your harp will fit in your pocket better." Andrew agreed. It felt better not to have to walk with a great big bulge digging at his hip. But he kept his hand over the harmonica there in his back pocket.

Aunt Tiny knew the taxi driver who was waiting outside her apartment.

"Big crowd tonight," he commented to Aunt Tiny.

"We got B. B. King," said Tiny proudly, as if she owned him. "And Koko Taylor. Going to be a heavy night tonight. Hope we don't get trampled."

Everybody laughed at the thought of Aunt Tiny being trampled. Andrew stored the bursting sound of their laugh to play later.

When they got to Grant Park, Aunt Tiny walked right up to the front of the big long line. She didn't slide to the middle of the line the way Yolonda did. Aunt Tiny smiled her wide, sweet smile, at one of the big men guarding the entrance.

"Hello, Eddie," she said. She gave him one of her smothering hugs.

"Hi, gorgeous!" The man liked the hug. He hugged back. He had huge arms and a big, warm smile, too. If you were big like this Eddie man, thought Andrew, or like Yolonda, you didn't get your breath stuffed back in by Aunt Tiny's hugs.

Andrew was pushed through the gate first, ahead of Yolonda. Today, the stamp was purple. Bleeding purple ink across the back of his hand were those reading marks. Andrew noticed the big

B for *bongos*—*B* for the *Blue* of Andrew—*B* for *blues*. With surprise he understood the runny purple stamp.

"*B* for *blues*," he said softly.

"I know all these college boys," bragged Tiny. "Most of their mommas come to one of my shops. Good boys."

She smiled at another tall, strong-muscled guard wearing a T-shirt with the sleeves rolled up tight against his wide upper arms. Yolonda muttered to the top of Andrew's head, "Hunk! Oh, what a hunk-o."

Their momma carried her camera with the long lens. At their seats she sat and focused on the stage. "I bet I can pick up the hair on B. B. King's upper lip with this thing," she said. "Color film at one thousand speed. Won't even need a flash."

Aunt Tiny began to offer around food from a big hamper. Yolonda took a piece of chicken and a napkin. Andrew wasn't hungry, but he thought of the big arms on the guards and how the Eddie man had hugged Tiny back, so he chose a croissant.

While he took bites, Andrew watched the crew on the great big stage, where they were setting up instruments. A grand piano was rolled in and uncovered. Drums were set in place.

There were lots of noises. Andrew knew that

soon the music people would come out onto the stage. They would look so little up there and there would be a hush-hush around them and then there would be a signal. And Andrew remembered that, like when insects stop singing all at once and the grass goes quiet, all of a sudden like that, the noises would pause.

The music people would reach up with their instruments or reach down to them and pull sounds to them and out through their horns or their guitars or the piano. They would push sound into bright pictures or smooth it into long paths. The noise would become a special shape that was wonderful to follow.

Andrew checked for his harmonica, safe in his back pocket. Yolonda looked at him and smiled, patting her pocket where he knew the case sat amid her supply of malt balls. Then his sister went back to looking at a creased paper filled with pictures and reading.

Just then a music man came on the stage. Aunt Tiny said very loud, "Go on, Jimmy Rogers, go on."

The Jimmy man had a guitar. He sang, "Got my mojo wukin'." The crowd clapped and laughed. "Got my mojo wukin'." The crowd sang with him. "Got my mojo wukin'." The crowd stood, hundreds of pointing fingers jabbed at the stage. "Got my mojo wukin'." The crowd cried out, "Mojo wukin'!" Some people got up and danced in the aisles.

Andrew was just about to pull out his harmonica and join the tumult of sound when Yolonda grabbed his hand. "Come on," she said in an urgent voice. "Got your Marine Band?" Andrew nodded. She guided him carefully past Aunt Tiny.

"What a time to leave," said Tiny.

"Yolonda. Where are you off to now?" snapped their momma. Andrew could play that short, tight sound.

"Bathroom break," said Yolonda. No arguments there.

Andrew felt the waves of Yolonda's energy propelling them up several aisles and out the security gate. He didn't have to go to the bathroom. Through the crowded street they marched. Yolonda took big long steps. They weren't going to the bathroom after all. A journey, thought Andrew with a mixture of excitement and worry. Are we ever coming back?

Yolonda was singing under her breath, "Got my mojo wukin'." At the end of the street, his big sister guided him to a bench near a row of tables under a yellow-and-white awning. She sat him down. "This is a lucky bench, Andrew. This is our lucky bench."

Andrew wiggled on the bench, trying to feel the luck. He listened for the sound of luck.

His sister was talking, still in her urgent voice. She had so many voices, and Andrew had a place on his harmonica for most of them. This voice was like the sound of the wind that pushed against you on a roller coaster.

". . . It's like a game. We're not really going to be lost. But we need to get backstage. Where the big-time musicians are. Where all those *instruments* are like the ones you ask about all the time. Would you like to go backstage?"

She was asking him something he didn't quite understand. He could only look at her, listening for a clue in her voice.

"I don't think we have to actually go onto the stage. Momma would faint dead away. I'll think of a way to get us out of there before that comes. Although . . ." Yolonda's face softened.

Andrew watched expectantly. Yolonda had magic; she could make things happen. *Got my mojo wukin'!* Mojo was a magic charm. Some people, like Yolonda, *were* mojos—could work magic without any extra help.

"Although . . . what would that be like? Sixty thousand people seeing you up on the stage? Calling out to you, clapping their hands, all crazy."

"Good?" asked Andrew.

"First things first," said Yolonda.

CHAPTER SEVENTEEN

The temporary police post was housed in a big CHICAGO POLICE motor van, white with sky-blue trim. Yolonda didn't want to start her plan there—too obvious. Half a block away, past a hot dog booth, were two cops talking together. One was a short, compact black woman whose uniform fit as if it had been sprayed on. Yolonda quelled the worry that she might not be able to fool a sister—that somehow this woman might be able to read her soul. The other cop was a young white guy with a pale mustache. He looked easy.

Yolonda checked Andrew. "Don't get worried,"

she said to him. He looked at her curiously, but his eyes were trusting as always.

Yolonda mustered her terrified-but-innocent look, grabbed Andrew's hand more tightly. She tried to shrink down inside the lace-collared blouse. With wide eyes, she slowly crept by the chatting police. The effect was somewhat spoiled, she realized, by Andrew's bright interest in everything around him. But she couldn't risk worrying him into a frightened face. It might only screw up his playing mood.

The chatting police never once glanced at them.

Yolonda clutched Andrew more tightly, and he looked at her in alarm. "'S'okay," she growled at him. "Part of the game." She slowed her pace to that of a worm. Clutching and staring, she crawled back past the two cops. Their conversation was animated.

Some police officers, thought Yolonda angrily. Supposed to be alert to emergency. Supposed to smell disaster. What's our tax money going for? Chatting police officers. Wait till I'm chief of police.

Then, before she'd thought it through, she bought herself a hot dog. Andrew declined.

"What am I doing?" she muttered aloud. "Lost children are too worried to buy hot dogs." Well, she thought, maybe I bought it first, before we got lost. Maybe I'm so scared I don't even eat the hot dog now. Maybe I just clutch it.

Back they walked toward the two police officers, whose conversation showed no signs of slowing down. Yolonda clutched her hot dog, clutched her brother. She rounded out her eyes until she thought they might explode with innocence and terror. She looked right, left, all around—as if she were searching for someone. Her eyes were getting dry. She longed to take a bite of the hot dog, which was giving off a warm, spicy odor. But not eating the hot dog was helping her achieve a suffering expression. She managed a moan when she passed the two cops.

This time the one with the pale mustache glanced up. Yolonda almost tripped in eagerness. Then he went back to listening to the lady cop. Yolonda ground her teeth. She wanted to shout at them. Yo-yos! What's wrong with you? Didn't you get any training? Can't you spot lost children?

She took a deep breath. "One more time," she gritted at Andrew.

This time, her moan was real anguish. She dragged her feet. She clutched her hot dog. Andrew cried in protest as her grip tightened hard on his little fingers.

It was the lady cop who stopped talking and looked at them, who asked, "Have you lost your mother, kids?" And the most surprising thing happened.

Yolonda burst into tears. A real Niagara Falls.

They waited on comfy upholstered chairs in the back of the CHICAGO POLICE van. Despite the coolness outside, it was warm and stuffy in the van. After Yolonda recovered from the shock of actually crying, the time dragged minute by minute. The hot dog rumbled uncomfortably in her stomach. Andrew fell asleep leaning against the armrest. His perfect little mouth was open, drool collecting on the pink inside of his lower lip.

This is not working right, thought Yolonda. Andrew's body thinks it's bedtime. We can't wait two hours for them to take us onstage. The concert will be all over with.

When she stood up, Andrew stirred and woke.

"Gotta check something, Drew-de-drew," she said, and went up front to the open door. Andrew followed.

There were no police outside on this side of the van. Yolonda leaned out of the door. There were some of them around front talking with a mounted police officer who leaned from her fine big horse and pointed at something up the street.

"We're outa here," announced Yolonda, holding out her hand to Andrew. No one saw them leave.

Yolonda headed for the yellow-and-white

awning across the street. She wasn't sure what the next step in the big plan was, but she wanted to get closer to the goal.

A new set of hospitality ladies sat sternly at their tables, checking the passes of a short line of people. Yolonda's eyes zeroed in on a tall, straight-backed woman whose blond hairdo supported a beautiful straw hat. She appeared to be in a hurry even though she was standing still. Occasionally someone would aim a question her way and she would issue a command.

A real boss lady, thought Yolonda. She paused to gather her forces. At that moment, the boss lady turned impatiently and headed out of the gate toward the CHICAGO POLICE van they had just escaped from.

Yolonda took a breath—now or never—and stepped directly into the boss lady's path.

Boss lady halted. "Yes?" She was brimming with impatience.

"We're lost children," said Yolonda, her innocence stretched across her face. "We're supposed to go backstage."

"Oh!" blew out boss lady. She tossed her hands up, then dropped them, slapping against her sides. She turned and called out to one of the hospitality ladies under the awning.

"Esther, sit these kids backstage. They're lost.

Let Henry take care of it when this set is over."

It was as simple as that. The big pian had moved into place.

A thrill sent goose bumps up Yolonda's legs. She thought, I can do anything. I can look out for my baby brother. I can dance and fight. I bet I can even turn double Dutch ropes with Shirley-whirley. Why not? One thing I have down is timing.

I suppose I'll have to apologize to Shirley-whirley, she thought. Before we can begin to train. The sync part is important—the rhythm. You have to practice a lot if you want your hearts to beat together in perfect harmony.

The triumphant feeling followed Yolonda to the backstage entrance. And then deserted her.

Backstage was a huge corridor filled with people. No dressing rooms, no couches, no champagne. Disappointment replaced Yolonda's triumph. Where was the man with the foil-covered trays? People surged about them in a rush. Some wore earphones. Others lounged against a wall waiting or sat on folding chairs.

One guy looked like a big-time musician, but Yolonda didn't know him from Adam. Besides, he was a white guy. He wore a white and glittery cow-boy suit and a big white cowboy hat. He had a long earring in one ear that swayed and caught the light when he moved. He put one foot on a chair and leaned into his knee. He was listening to the group onstage and smiling, shaking his head.

Where was Koko Taylor? Little Willie Littlefield? Where was B. B. King? Yolonda found herself irritated by the cowboy musician's whiteness. Where was someone who would be turned on by Andrew's specialness?

Suddenly, into her mind slid a horrible doubt. Suppose she was wrong? Suppose everybody else was right? Suppose Andrew wasn't a genius after all—just an undersized underachiever? Where'd she gotten the idea he was a genius anyway? Desperately Yolonda's mind grabbed for the John Hersey definition—"rearranges old material . . ." She took a breath. Well, anyway, they were all about to find out.

There was quietness but hurrying in the tall place that seemed, to Andrew, like a hallway for giants. Lots of people were moving quickly and softly. They never bumped into one another. At the end of the hallway there was an edge of bright, bright light, and music sounds twinkled and faded, twinkled and faded.

One guy didn't move. He was standing with one foot on a chair. He wore a white cowboy hat and a long, sparkly earring. Andrew was more fascinated by the guitar that leaned against the chair. He moved closer. The instrument was white and sparkly, too. Andrew looked it over very carefully. He wondered where the guitar's case was. Wasn't this sparkly cowboy worried about his guitar?

Sounds seeped backstage from out front, where now a singer was sobbing, ". . . drivin' me-ah craze-eah. . . ." A slow, soft piano played behind her voice.

Without thinking, Andrew stepped closer to the stage entrance and pulled out his harmonica. He began to slide little notes in and out of the sounds around him.

He played a sparkle sound—the dazzling cowboy. He played the announcer man standing in the wings with his straw hat and his handful of papers. He played a deep bellowing sound—Yolonda hovering near.

"That there's some pretty fine sound, kid," said the sparkly cowboy behind Andrew. "You blowin' some good stuff outa that little harp, man."

Interrupted, Andrew turned to look at the cowboy. But, almost immediately, the guitar by the chair drew his eyes down. "You have to be big to play that," Andrew said. He smiled at the sparkly cowboy, raised up the Marine Band harmonica in a salute. *I don't have my case either.*

Yolonda seemed drawn, too, by the cowboy. She closed in on him.

"My little brother is a child prodigy," she announced. At least she didn't say *genius* again. Andrew's dislike for that word surfaced briefly.

"Believe it!" said the sparkly cowboy. "If I ain't mistaken, he was audiatin' a little just then. Who's he studyin' with?"

Audiating. Yolonda did that, too—used words that closed you in a box.

"I was not," he muttered into the harmonica. Then he played, *I was not, I was not!*

"Okay. Okay," said the sparkly cowboy.

Andrew was surprised. He never expected a stranger to answer the things his harmonica said—not with words anyway.

"He's not studying," said Yolonda. "He needs to study. He needs a teacher for a genius. Know anyone?"

There was that word again.

"Is he playin' tonight?" asked the cowboy.

"No," said Yolonda. Andrew saw that she looked startled. "We're lost children."

The sparkly cowboy laughed. "This kid ain't lost, sister. You don't look like you lost either. Sure he ain't with one'a the groups?"

"He oughta be," said Yolonda. "Maybe he oughta be going out on that stage—instead of some others around here."

Why is she so mad? wondered Andrew.

Then the sound of his sister sharpened even more. "We're looking for Koko Taylor. We're looking for B. B. King. I need to talk to somebody who can listen to my genius kid brother."

Andrew could suddenly hear his own heart. Was that why they were here?

"He's worth listening to, awright," said the cowboy. He smiled down at Andrew. Andrew felt a scary warmness flooding through him.

His sister glared at the sparkly cowboy. "There's a lot of stuff he needs to learn, and he needs the best kind of teacher to show him."

The cowboy had half a smile looking at Yolonda.

Yolonda said, "Takes more than a fancy suit to play great blues. Great blues musicians don't need a whole lot of glitter."

Whole lot of glitter, played Andrew on the Marine Band harmonica. He gave it a mean edge like Yolonda's voice had right now. He was trying to figure out the heavy pushing that came from her like the push that came from big trucks—the trucks that broke up cement. He played the cement-breaking truck. Then he mixed in the bustle and short snap of voices in the corridor. He sent the sound out to meet the music that drifted back to him with the faint burning buzz of the crowd. He played the sudden silence of his sister and the sparkly cowboy.

Well, thought Yolonda, no problem getting Andrew to play. He's on fire tonight.

Andrew stopped playing, but the listening stayed in his eyes.

"You are right about your kid brother, gal," said the cowboy, leaning toward Yolonda and looking her straight in the face. "But you don't have to be jealous of my pretty costume."

Yolonda glared. "I want the *right* people to hear my brother," she said. "Somebody's got to see what he is besides me."

Then the cowboy musician did something that startled Yolonda into silence. He smiled; he put his arm around her powerful shoulders and he gave her a nudge of a hug.

"You got a gift yourself, girl," he said. "It comes in a mean sorta package, but it's a gift all right."

Yolonda glared at the cowboy. But no words, big or small, came to her mind.

"Well, hello there, Davie Rae," said a voice behind them—a silver voice, resonant and smooth as a deep bell.

Yolonda turned and saw someone as familiar as her father. She stared. Her mind scrabbled for facts—then knew. It was Mr. B. B. King, the Blues Boy himself. He looked like a real person.

"Whatcha got there? New band member?" B. B. King cocked his wide, smiling face at

Andrew. He wore glasses, not like in his pictures.

"Maybe so, Beeb, maybe so," said the cowboy musician. "He gotta have a tutor. Know anyone wantsa take on a pro-gidy? A pro-digy—whatever?"

"Prodigy, Davie Rae. Prodigy," said B. B. King. "Lemme hear the kid, Davie; lemme hear him do his stuff."

"Thought we might throw him to the crowd," said the Davie Rae cowboy, and he winked at Yolonda.

Davie Rae? Davie Rae Shawn? Yolonda winced. He was featured on the program. Must be somebody special. She groaned. What had she said to him? Well, what of it? He liked her, she could tell. And he'd noticed Andrew's playing. And now— what had he said? Throw Andrew to the crowd? Wait a minute. Wait just a *minute*!

CHAPTER EIGHTEEN

There was no stopping things now. She had set something in motion and it was all suddenly moving too fast. She couldn't even slow it down. Musicians with instruments were coming and going in the corridor.

Yolonda tried to make herself as small and innocent and lost-looking as possible as she followed Andrew out onto the vast stage. The lights were so hard and bright that she winced.

She certainly couldn't let Andrew march out with Davie Rae Shawn all by himself. Her brother had turned his face inquiringly to Yolonda when this Shawn guy had said, "That's a good name for a harp man, Andrew Blue." He had put his hand against Andrew's back to guide him onstage. "You'll be a whole different intro for the boys. They need t'be shook up every so often."

Was Andrew actually going to introduce the band? How? Did Shawn want him to talk? Or play? Did he just want to get sympathy from the crowd with this cute little black kid standing there?

As if pulled by an invisible string, Yolonda kept pace behind Shawn and Andrew. She hung on to the lost-child routine. It gave her a reason for being there. Now that she actually stood on the stage, it seemed as big as an airfield. She couldn't see anything except a wall of lights. But there was a grim and horrible roar from the darkness beyond the footlights and the overhead spots—like a great, writhing monster. The monster gave off a shimmering energy as it continually changed its shape. Yolonda became small and lost without even trying.

The microphone sent the MC's voice out over the monster, which paused in its writhing.

"We have here two lost children," said the MC.

Davie Rae Shawn eyed Yolonda.

"Two lost kids—but their loss is our gain, folks." The MC waved his arm toward Andrew. "This little dude here, I'm told, is a mean harp man. Two lost kids—one found musician. Somewhere out

there among you folks is a worried momma."
There was a murmuring in the crowd. "Just hang
in there, momma. Your kids are safe."

Yolonda groaned. A crazy-mad momma would be
more accurate. She tried to peer through the sheet
of light.

"Now—without further ado, lemme also introduce you folks out there to a *me-e-ean* young guitar
man come all the way from the big state of Texas.
Folks, let's give a Chicago welcome to Davie Rae
Shawn!"

The monster beyond the lights began to howl
and whistle. Yolonda could feel the energy come in
a rush toward them, and she instinctively braced
herself. Part of her thought, This Shawn guy must
be Big-time big-time. Another part wondered
where in the monster of movement and murmur-
ings were her momma and Aunt Tiny.

Davie Rae Shawn leaned into his own mike.
"Don' you worry, Mrs. Blue. Your kids're safe. An'
y'all out there—y'all gonna hear some new kinda
sounds. How 'bout it for li'l Andrew Blue!" And
the cowboy musician dove into his guitar and shot
out some crazy chords.

Yolonda felt a thrill of fear and hopelessness
wash through her. Andrew *was* little. There was
nothing more she could do now. He was a little
six-year-old kid with a Marine Band harmonica on

a stage for giants, and he was on his own.

"And what would you like to play for us, Mr. Andrew Blue?" asked Davie Rae. He swung a microphone down until it was level with Andrew's head. Then he stepped back and fastened his guitar over his shoulder.

Yolonda saw the sax man moisten the reed of his saxophone. She pulled in a deep lungful of Chicago air.

"This is Yolonda," said Andrew, and the mike tossed his little-boy voice out to the crowd: *"This is Yolonda."*

At first Yolonda thought he was introducing her, and she blew out her breath in shock. The whole campaign of her own conniving seemed dreadful, and she hung suspended for a long and terrible moment as Andrew, like a slow-motion dream, lifted the harmonica to his lips.

He played a few warm-up chords, testing the sound as it was sucked into the microphone and thrown into the dark lake of people. He paused, listening to it, surprised.

Then Andrew drew his harmonica from his mouth and put it back into his pocket. From the neck of his shirt, he pulled out the little wooden pipe. He placed his fingers, his mouth against the pipe and, like a proper beginning, he blew his waking-up song. But different. Such sadness in it.

Sweet and clean and sad the sound sailed out over the crowd, out over Lake Michigan to join the boats rocking at their moorings. The sound hovered still when Andrew dropped the pipe and reached for his harmonica. The monster beyond the footlights waited, hypnotized.

We are all covered with light, thought Andrew, like angels in Bible pictures. His listening reached through the lights. He could hear the great breath and motion of thousands of people out there in the dark beyond. The microphone bending down was mojo. And he knew the sky was there and that insects fluttered in tunnels of light sent onto the stage. Glimmering in the distance were the great buildings of Chicago's skyline.

The lights were warm on him and a cool breeze wafted across him, cooling—warming—cooling. Andrew closed his eyes, his mind stretching out to his sister at the edge of the stage. *She had cried in front of the police people*. Now something unfamiliar came to him from Yolonda. It made him uneasy. Then he knew. Yolonda is afraid, he thought, and the idea was so awful that he felt for a moment as if he were falling. *No!*

No. *This is Yolonda*. And he told them—all those people out behind the lights—"*This* is Yolonda."

He had to play his morning wake-up song—to

gentle the mike, call his sister back. To let the sadness go. After that, he needed his harmonica. For the mike—for the big voice like a giant.

The feel of the wood and metal in his hands, against his mouth, steadied everything. Shapes of sounds he had been thinking about for weeks fell together. He pushed his breath into them.

Yolonda walking, a steady, strong beat—great big moves, slow, making waves of air pass by. Yolonda eating a chocolate éclair—full mouth—soft and happy. Yolonda reading to him, voice purring around the big words. Yolonda dancing. This is the sound of Yolonda's body— large, gobbling space, powerful and protecting—great like a queen, frightening everyone with a scowl and a swelling of her shoulders.

Behind Andrew came a whisper of snares as the drummer joined the song of Yolonda.

Then Andrew played a sweet, rich sound, smooth as Yolonda's skin, dark and shiny as her eyes. The bass viol began a soft thumping, and the guitar came in deep.

Andrew felt his sound carried up and out over the dark lake of people. Farther out, the greater Lake Michigan held the moon. Andrew played the moon. The sparkly cowboy was humming softly along with his guitar. The saxophone and now the piano joined together behind Andrew, carried him up and up. The dark sky had no end.

So Andrew slipped his harmonica into his belt and put the pipe to his mouth. He played a high, wrenching note. Then he blew a long note that leaned and spread—a single note that seemed to reach back through hundreds of years. *Yolonda. Big Sister! Big queen in the world.*

The guitar of Davie Rae Shawn picked up the theme, joining Andrew. *Yolonda. Sister! Queen in the world!*

Yolonda found her mouth open. The monster had loosened and separated itself into faces of people, hands waving, cheering and clapping. Several flash-bulbs sent out shocks of light. She sure hoped her momma's astonishment had worn off soon enough for her to be getting this on that one-thousand-speed film.

"Andrew Blue!" announced Davie Rae Shawn into the microphone, reminding the crowd. Andrew listened for a moment to the cheering. He waved his Marine Band harmonica at them. Then he walked across the stage, small shape against a sea of partially lit faces, a tiny fish, swimming sure and confident to his big, oh-so-big and grand whale of a sister. He put his small hand in her large one and looked out into the crowd.

The crowd kept up a furious applause. "Yeah, awright, yeah!"

Yolonda's mind was swimming. What next? But she nodded her head faintly in acknowledgment at the crowd—the way she'd seen the queen of England do at a parade in her honor.

The MC chortled into the mike. "Is this the finest blues city in the world? Let's all give a round of applause for a brand-new Chicago musician— Mr. Andrew Blue!"

How dumb, thought Yolonda. The crowd was already clapping their hands off. Besides, Andrew didn't belong to Chicago. They lived in Grand River. Then, through the noise and all the strangeness, her good instincts took over. It was time to go. Leave 'em hungry, she thought.

She took Andrew's hand, turned. She didn't shake off the thousands of eyes that were certainly fastened to their backs. Andrew tucked his harmonica into his pocket, the pipe under his shirt.

Yolonda paced their exit—slow, but not too slow—toward the giant stage's shadowy wings, where she could see lights winking from Mr. B. B. King's glasses. One thing this girl has down, she thought, is timing.

They left Chicago late that night, after hearing Mr. B. B. King play an amazing final set, after hustling through the still-cheering crowd, lugging Aunt Tiny's hamper and pillows. Their momma had packed the car earlier that day. They rushed through last-minute checks for scattered things in Tiny's apartment, rushed through hugs and promises. Their momma needed to get home to prepare for work the next day. Her usual hurrying state had returned.

From the time they left the crystal twinkle of Chicago lights, during the whole three-hour drive, Yolonda's brain whirled, carrying the night's events in her head like objects in a tornado:

Her momma's face, filled with joy and scolding, as she rushed up East Jackson Street to claim her children.

"Didja get any pictures?" Yolonda had put her momma on the defensive before she could start a tirade. "And Mr. B. B. King wants you to call him." She let that land like a bomb.

"Yolonda, you are an astonishment," said her momma, "and you try me to the teeth."

A reporter from the *Sun-Times* had halted their exit to get "a close-up of the kid" and some information from their mother. There was nothing for their momma to do but go with the flow. Aunt Tiny kept turning to people, bragging about "my nephew—that itty-bitty boy child."

The hum of their car mingled with the sounds in Yolonda's dozing brain. Mr. B. B. King's silver voice: *". . . doesn't have enough of the hunger in him—or the hormones, yet—to blow the range of the blues. Got the sad though, Miss . . .? Yolonda, you say. Well, Yolonda, he's rare. A thinker. And he has the touch, the gift. Girl, he really has the gift! But he's a thinker. Jazz, maybe. Intellectual like that. Or classical. Does he read music?"*

Andrew had told Mr. B. B. King, "I'm learning the Mickey Mouse feet." And Mr. B. B. King had laughed and laughed before he explained to Yolonda what Andrew meant. I should have known, thought Yolonda.

All the way home, through the foggy sleepiness that came and went, she checked (or dreamed she checked) her pocket for the card with B. B. King's number on it.

"Have your folks call me, Yolonda. I'd like to keep track of this young man."

The great gloomy weight had lifted. She could share Andrew with everybody now. She couldn't wait to tell Shirley about Andrew and the Chicago Blues Festival.

An image of Shirley marching away with the loops of rope over her shoulder shot briefly into her mind.

I have the whole summer, thought Yolonda. Shirley would love to hear about Davie Rae Shawn and B. B. King and all. About Andrew and the glory of being onstage. Blow by blow she would tell Shirley about the workings of her big plan. After they made up, of course.

Briefly, her mind wrestled with face-saving approaches. Then she thought, I don't have to do that. Better to start out on the right foot, even if it's harder. Best friends should trust each other.

"I'd like to apologize . . ." she would begin.

THE CHICAGO MUSIC FESTIVALS

My husband and I have been going to both the jazz and blues festivals in Chicago's Grant Park for over ten years. For the purposes of the book, I have lumped together some of the happenings at both festivals, but I chose the blues festival to focus on because, although I think Andrew's music might lend itself better to jazz, June was a better month, from the logistical standpoint of the book, for them to return to Chicago.

I have also lumped together the festivals as they have been experienced by me over the years. Changes in methods of crowd control, times of concerts, schedule of musicians, and the mayoral administration make each festival somewhat different. What may appear to be questionable facts are the facts as I have gathered them over many years. I was more interested in capturing the overall feeling of the huge free festivals in Grant Park in all their sprawling splendor.

I saw the girl who became Yolonda with her little brother onstage between sets at one of the early jazz festivals. She looked too big, too old, and too competent to be a lost child. She stayed in my mind, her face unsmiling and only a little intimidated by the enormity of the crowd looking at her.

Carol Fenner